Hard Desires

Sexy Stories Collection

VOLUME 46

3 EROTIC NOVELLAS

SHALA BREECE

Publisher's Note: This is a work of fiction. Names, characters, places, and incidents are a product of the author's imagination. Locales and public names are sometimes used for atmospheric purposes. Any resemblance to actual people, living or dead, or to businesses, companies, events, institutions, or locales is completely coincidental.

Hard Desires/ Shala Breece. -- 1st ed.
Xplicit Press, an imprint of TLM Media LLC

ISBN-13: 978-1-62327-577-8
ISBN-10: 1-62327-577-6
eISBN: 978-1-62327-627-0

Printed in the United States of America

CONTENTS

1	The Man With The Chocolate Rod	1
2	His Personal Sexetary	57
3	Torn: Sacrifices Of A Vampire Prince	113

1 THE MAN WITH THE CHOCOLATE ROD

Flipping her cell phone open once more, with shaky fingers Kesha dialed his number for the fifth time that night. *Why did she even put up with this?* she wondered to herself. There were so many men who were vying for her love and affection, all just as handsome as Kevin. In fact, some of her suitors were even more handsome and charming than her current boyfriend. She could be equally as happy with any of these men. However, it seemed like every time Kesha got ready to break up with Kevin and move on, he would pull her right back into the situation. The truth was that he was an amazing lover. The sex with him was always so great that she would be angry one minute and in sweet ecstasy the next, having totally forgotten that she'd ever been angry.

Kesha Whitfield was a gorgeous black

woman; her chocolate brown complexion was the envy of many of her friends. She had beautiful hazel eyes and two rows of perfect white teeth. And she had a great job, working as a lawyer at one of Miami's top law firms. Her boyfriend Kevin Bradford was equally as handsome. Unlike her, he had light caramel complexion that complemented her darker chocolate complexion well. To people on the outside, the two of them seemed like the perfect couple: they would go out fishing together; he would hold her bags at the mall; he would even occasionally go to the spa with her to get massages done together. However, as their relationship progressed, things took a turn for the worst around their four-year anniversary.

Kevin changed. He began coming home late, taking his phone calls outside; there were even times when she would wake up in the middle of the night to an empty bed. She usually had no idea where he was going when he left the house, and if she asked his answer was always, "I'm going to work dear. I work for myself, remember, so I need to work extra hard to make that dough." Then he would leave, expecting her to understand.

Tonight was a typical example of how Kevin just did not care. *How can you leave your home and have your phone switched off?* she thought to herself. One last time, she dialed his number, keeping her fingers, crossed hoping that he would pick up her call. It went straight to voicemail.

"Hi you've reached Kevin. Sorry, I can't come to the phone. I'm busy either with my girlfriend

Kesha or at work. Leave your name and number and I'll call you back."

How ironic, she thought to herself; there he was saying he was busy with her, while she was here trying to reach him. Looking at the huge clock that hanged on the wall to her left, she realized that it was now two in the morning. Where could her boyfriend be this late? And why was he not answering his phone?

As she watched the time pass, her blood boiled and she found herself getting angrier and angrier. Several thoughts lingered in her mind. More than ever, she was convinced that he was cheating on her. How could he? Although they didn't have a perfect relationship, she thought it was pretty solid in terms of their commitment to each other. She surely was not out at all hours of the night, and she was definitely not seeing or talking to any other guy. Finally, after pacing back and forth in the living room worried about what he was doing or, worse, *whom* he was doing, Kesha dropped down on the couch and let her emotions get the best of her. Her face was buried in her hands as she cried her eyes out. Suddenly she felt a gentle pat on her shoulders; looking up with swollen eyes, she saw Kevin standing next to her.

"Where you coming from, Kevin?" she shrieked pulling viciously against his touch. He reached around his back where he had been hiding a bouquet of vibrant red roses.

"I'm sorry. I got caught up at the office in a meeting. Then we went for drinks with the client."

Looking at the clock, Kesha replied, "You had drinks until three in the morning, Kevin? That's what you want me to believe?"

Kevin stood there with a straight face and refused to change his story, saying that he was telling the truth and had no reason to lie to her. Finally, Kesha gave up and brushed passed him, making her way upstairs to her room.

She'd been in a deep sleep when suddenly she felt something between her legs. It grew more intense and pleasurable. She was now moaning to sensation of whatever was happening between her thighs. As she opened her eyes, she saw Kevin's head below. It finally dawned on her that he was sucking her pussy.

"Kevin, stop," she said breathlessly, still very upset with him.

"Shh... Don't speak, just enjoy," he whispered to her as he used his finger to part her pussy lips and his tongue lavished the insides.

She would have tried to resist again but she was too weak with desire to do anything but moan. His tongue felt so good on her flesh. He was an excellent lover when it came to oral sex; he would be able to make her orgasm in matter of minutes. Tonight was no different. As he flicked his tongue back and forth on her clit she found herself begging for more as her juices trickled down her cunt. He changed his focus from the slit of her pussy to her clit, taking it into his mouth with great vigor and sucking on it hard. He then eased the grip he had on her clitoris and gently massaged it with his tongue. Kesha gave a loud moan as he left her clit and plunged his tongue inside her moist heat. He teased her insides with his tongue and she found it almost unbearable.

Gripping firmly onto his hair, she locked his head down on her flesh. Her reaction motivated him to increase the momentum with which he was tongue fucking her, plunging his tongue faster inside her pussy.

"Oh God, yes" she moaned as she bucked her pussy against his lips.

He happily continued to stroke her insides with his tongue, giving her slow gentle strokes at first followed by faster, more intense strokes. Her pleasure increased and her body quivered at the touch of his desire-filled tongue. With a loud moan, she summited her climax and exploded on his tongue. He continued licking and sucking on her flesh, as if trying to take in all her sweet juices. When he was done, he mounted her, missionary-style.

His lips met her mouth and as he gently sucked on her lower lip, Kesha found her body aching for him to penetrate her. The delirium of the moment had whipped away any thoughts of anger that she had towards him. His tongue danced with hers as their bodies braced against each other. Finally, she felt his dick slowly entering her tunnel of love. She closed her eyes as his massive cock tore through her flesh, forcing it to expand to accommodate him. A loud moan escaped her lips as he plunged his entire length deep inside her with a single thrust. He was no longer being gentle; his cock rammed inside her cunt viciously and she had no choice but to grip his shoulders and enjoy the ride. As he fucked her, Kesha pussy became warmer and more inviting as tiny spasms made their way down from the middle of her spine to the center of her womanhood.

He gave her a combination of slow, gentle thrusts and harder, quicker thrusts. Their bodies moved together perfectly as she lost herself in the euphoric moment. Kevin increased his momentum and was now ramming his shaft deep down inside her pussy.

"Oh God, Kevin. Don't stop," she moaned as he plummeted inside her over and over. Finally, with a loud thunderous groan, he exploded his load of cum deep down in her pussy. She, too, was on the brink of her climax, and released her sea of cum on his dick. He continued to thrust inside her as his dick shot out its hot liquid. When he was done, he fell beside her and they both dozed off.

The following morning Kesha got up and left for work as she normally did. At the office, her day had been going well when her secretary called her informing her that there was a Miss Davis there to see her. Kesha worked at a prestigious law firm where almost all her clients made appointments before coming to her office. It was a bit weird that this woman would just walk in and request to see her. If she had been busier she would have asked her to come back, but her workload at that moment was light and she decided to let her come in.

As she sat at her desk, there was a knock at the door. Kesha called out, giving them permission to enter. A pregnant woman walked in. She had blonde hair and looked like she was in her early thirties, a little younger than Kesha who would turn thirty-six in a few weeks. The two of them exchanged greetings and Kesha extended her hand out to the stranger, who refused to be pleasant with her.

"Miss Whitfield," she said with an intense gaze at Kesha. "I don't know what's going on between you and my fiancé, and I just came here to tell you to stay away from my man. We're about to start a family, as you can clearly see," she said, rubbing her belly.

Kesha almost laughed in the woman's face. She took a moment to collect her thoughts before responding. "Your man?" was all that came out; it almost sounded like a rhetorical question.

Had this woman not been with child, Kesha would have thrown her out of her office in an instant. She'd never felt so disrespected in her life. However, as she stood there her anger began to subside and she could not help but feel sorry for this pitiful woman. *What kind of man cheats on their pregnant fiancée?* she thought to herself.

Clearly, this woman must have her mistaken for someone else. She looked at the woman with compassion in her eyes.

"Don't do this to my baby. I don't care how

long y'all been together, just leave him alone, please. I don't want to raise this baby alone," the woman was almost pleading with Kesha at that point.

There was a look of sincerity in her deep green eyes. Kesha had to clear the air; she was definitely not a home wrecker and Kevin was definitely not the man that this woman was talking about. She had heard of women who had been confronted at work by other women about a cheating man, but Kesha never thought she would find herself in that type of situation. Oh no, not her. She was a professional woman who was in a good, stable relationship. Although she had had her doubts about Kevin, she did not believe that he would have a fiancée, much less a pregnant one. No, this woman could not be talking about her Kevin.

"Listen, Ms...?" she said while looking at the woman to get her name.

"It's Mrs. Bradford. The wedding will be in the next six months, so you may as well address me by that name." There was a slight hint of arrogance in her voice.

"Mrs. Bradford!" Kesha exclaimed in disbelief. She still did not believe that the woman was referring to her boyfriend. *There could be many people with Bradford as their last name,* she thought to herself, trying to comfort herself.

"You must have mistaken me for someone else. I don't even know who you're talking about. I am not seeing anybody else's man," Kesha replied, walking around to where the woman was standing. "I hope you do find who you're looking for because both your fiancé and this other woman deserve a good ass whooping," she said jokingly, trying to break the tension in the room.

The woman looked tentatively at Kesha trying to determine whether she was just lying or really naïve. Then with an intense look in her eye, she replied to Kesha. "So you're telling me you don't know Kevin Bradford? Right? Cause that's my fiancé and baby daddy."

Kesha's mouth dropped open and she gasped in disbelief. "Who? Kevin Bradford, the photographer?"

The woman nodded her head. "Yes, that's exactly who I'm talking about. He drives a gray Ford truck, and his office is at 180 Sheridan Street, Homer."

At that moment, it dawned on Kesha and her world came crashing down. The late night phone calls, the creeping in, and the disappearing in the middle of the night – it was all starting to make sense. Kevin had been leaving a double life. Kesha kept true to herself and remained calm. She had always said that if she were to ever find out Kevin had been cheating on her; she would deal with Kevin and not his mistress. From the look on Kesha's face, the other woman realized that she was just a victim of Kevin's deceitfulness.

Although Kesha was able to maintain some control, she could not stop the stream of tears that had made it down along her cheeks. How could Kevin embarrass her like this? Here she was at work, having a good day, thinking that everything was all good between them, only to be presented with this shocking revelation. She felt her blood boil and the urgency to confront Kevin became uncontrollable. She picked up her phone and dialed his number. Unlike last night, he picked up the call. He sounded happy to hear from her but she did not return his enthusiasm. She asked him if she could drop by and he was readily agreed.

Kesha had him on speaker phone the entire time so the other woman could hear, just to confirm in her mind that it was really her Kevin. The woman told her that was Kevin's voice on the other end of the line, and she called out Kevin's number to prove that she knew his voice.

The other woman joined her as they went down to the parking lot to get her car. She was going to go over to his office and confront him with his mistress standing right there. Kevin worked as a photographer and had a small art studio in the city. As they knocked on the door, he invited them in. His jaw dropped suddenly when he saw the other woman.

"Gale!" he gasped, placing his hand over his mouth in disbelief.

He did not get the chance to say anything else or explain himself; Kesha pounced on him, delivering several hard blows to the back his head and face. At that moment, she did not care that she could catch a case by hitting him. All she wanted to do was hurt him as much as he had hurt her. He had his hand over his head trying to block her attack, and was wailing at the other woman to leave so that he could talk to Kesha. It took all he had to finally grab hold of Kesha's hand and pacify her.

He apologized profusely about putting her in such a position. However, Kesha was not having any of it. This was the last straw. Out of all the mean and hurtful things he had ever done to her, this was by far the worst. “How could you do this to me Kevin?” she shrieked as she delivered another set of hard blows to his temple. Again, he was able to get her off him, but his time he walked over to the window behind a huge table to widen the gap between Kesha and himself.

He told her that Gale was his ex-girlfriend and he had gone back to have a one-night stand with her, a night when he and Kesha had had a huge fight. A few weeks after he had sex with Gale she called him and told him she was pregnant. He did not believe her at first because in the past she had used so many false baby alarms on him it was hard to keep track. All he knew was that she wanted him back and she would do anything to get him. He tried to prove what he was saying by pointing out that Gale had gone all the way to Kesha’s office just to stir up some drama.

“She wants us to break up, baby, can’t you see that?” he asked in a pleading tone of voice.

He begged her to take him back, saying that Gale’s baby was definitely not his, he was one hundred per cent sure of that. Kesha did not want to believe him, but he had a certain charm about him; he could look down into her eyes and cause her to melt. Gradually her body began to calm down. Kevin looked outside the window and could see Gale hailing a cab at the street corner. He swiftly walked across to where Kesha was standing and captured her lips with his.

Kesha wanted to resist him, but as usual, she found herself giving in to his gentle, passionate kisses. He pulled her in close to him and pinned her back against the wall. His hands were now exploring her body.

"Wait," he said as his left her hungry lips and he across the room to lock the doors and shut the blinds.

He turned to her and took her lips in one more time. This time he kissed her with so much vigor that she could barely remain steady. His hands roamed along her body, cupping her breasts as he fondled them through the fabric of her dress. She'd been wearing a black casual work dress that hugged her curvaceous body perfectly. She had always had a great figure – perking full breasts, a narrow waist and a round bum. As they kissed, his hand soon left her breasts and made their way down along the zipper in the back of her dress, causing her apparel to fall to the floor, exposing her bare skin. Kesha could feel the coolness of the A/C on her flesh. She was almost naked. She'd been wearing red lingerie beneath her clothes and now that Kevin's eyes had caught her sexy underwear, there was an instant spark in his eyes. He pulled back a little and his eyes travelled up and down her body taking in her beauty.

"What?" she teased.

"You look amazing, that's all," he said, his voice hoarse as he pulled her in with a passionate kiss.

This time his kisses were slow and full of

desire. Their tongues danced in sweet ecstasy and their bodies ached for each other. He loosed the bra and just as it slid off her body, her breasts popped free. He immediately seized her nipple with his hot mouth, causing her to let out a soft moan. His tongue stroked the dark chocolate nipples while his hand fondled her free breasts. He pulled away from their embrace one last time, scooping her up in his arm and walking over to his desk.

He sat her on the edge of the huge oak desk, propping her legs up and then parting them. She was still wearing her panties and that bothered him a little. He quickly pulled them up to her hoisted knees and then down her rest of her leg. Parting her legs further, his head dove into her core.

"Oh baby, yeah" her voice had a tone of urgency and longing in it.

His tongue had made contact with her bare flesh. Her pussy was wet, wetter than he had expected it to be. It had sent a shiver through his body when he tasted her moistness on his tongue. He quickly propped her leg further back, giving him better access to her pink flesh.

"Don't stop, just like that. Oh God!" Her hands had gripped the edge of the desk for support. He wanted to plunge his entire face inside her warmness. His tongue probed her insides as his dick throbbed in anticipation of fucking her. The whole idea of having sex in the office had always aroused him. He loved seeing her on his desk, jerking back and forth, trying hard to control herself while his massive cock destroyed her tight snatch. He worked his tongue up from her dripping wet slit to her swollen clit. Her clit was the biggest juiciest clit he'd ever. He could suck on it for hours and was always amazed at how big it would swell up. Taking the clit in his mouth, he gave it some slow succulent sucks, massaging the very tip of it with his tongue. The more he sucked her there, the more her body quivered; her legs were now shaky as she panted hard, trying to hold onto to her release as long as she could.

He knew exactly how to make her cum. He released the tight grip he had on her clit and changed his strategy. He was now flicking his tongue wildly over her clitoris. His tongue searched down her wet pussy and found the narrow opening. Without warning, he plunged his tongue inside the hole, flicking it on the insides. She moaned even more now that she was reaching her climax. Her body twisted and turned to the feel of his tongue as she let out a long loud moan. He tasted her juices rushing down on his tongue. Satisfied that he had pleasured her fully, he stepped back and whipped out his huge cock, stroking it a few times.

Kesha slipped down on her knees and took hold of him in her mouth. He gasped as her tongue lavished his dick. Her tongue was hot and wet over his raw meat and he found himself gripping firmly to the back of her head guiding her mouth on him. She sucked on him with so much life, and the power of her suctions had him weak in the knees. He was groaning out in pure pleasure. Suddenly she increased the momentum of her strokes; her tongue was now brutal on his cock. The more she sucked the closer he came to exploding his load of cum in her mouth. But he tried hard to resist the urge to release; he wanted to feel her moist cunt on his dick.

It took all his might to pull her mouth off his dick. He hoisted her onto the edge of the desk once more and parted her legs; this time he penetrated her with his erection. She tensed up a little, as if trying to take his full length in was too much for her tightness.

He pulled out his dick and gave another full thrust that caused her to jerk backwards a little. His dick was throbbing as he penetrated her wet pussy over and over. They both moaned in shared ecstasy as their emotions got the best of them. Thrust after thrust he gave her, some long and hard, others short and quick. Their bodies moved in perfect harmony.

But he wanted more; he wanted to make her ass bounce and ripple as he penetrated her. In a swift movement, he changed positions and bent her over the desk. Her ass was propped out facing him. He parted her ass cheeks and probed his dick along her pussy from the back. She was moaning as he teased her wetness.

Finally, he gave her a single thrust and his dick was inside her. He pulled his dick out half way and slammed it back inside her pussy. He felt tiny ripples run through her ass cheeks and vibrate against his dick. It made his arousal even more intense, and he gripped firmly onto her round bum and penetrated inside her moistness with several harder thrusts. Kesha was now moaning louder than ever as her body jerked forward repeatedly from the force of his thrusts.

The palm of his right hand made contact with her bare flesh, as he smacked her ass. She shrieked out in pain for the first few smacks, but eased off into the pleasure of having her ass smacked while her pussy was pounded. When he noticed that she was enjoying it all a little more than he had intended, he yanked on her silky black hair, pulling her body even closer to his. A sharp moan escaped her lips as he continued to serve her with several hard thrusts. Over and over, he penetrated her pussy, causing her juices to flow all over his dick. Finally, with a few very hard intense thrusts he exploded in her pussy. She continued to bounce her pussy on his dick until she cried out in ecstasy as she reached her climax.

As they finished putting their clothes back on, Kesha glanced at the watch on her wrist. “Oh damn, fuck, look at the time,” she said, scrambling to put on her black stilettos and then standing up and fixing her hair neatly into the ponytail it had been tucked neatly in before her heated office romancing. She did not spend too much time fixing her hair though, since she’d been out of her office for over two hours now. Grabbing her cell phone and her bag that was on the table beside her, she headed straight for the door.

“Wait,” he called out to her and took few strides towards her.

His hand cupped her face as he leaned in a planted a gentle kiss on her lips.

"Promise me, I have nothing to worry about Kevin?"

"I promise you have nothing to worry about; Gale's just trying to come between us. It was a one-night stand with her. She and I are done. Over. That baby she's carrying can't possibly be mine. I slept with her over a year ago."

Kevin kissed her again. This time there was more passion in his kiss. It was like he was trying to reassure her of what he'd just said. His kiss left her almost dizzy.

Taking in a deep breath, Kesha relented. "Well, okay, I'll give you the benefit of the doubt, baby," she said as she kissed him one last time and walked out the door.

When she got back to her office Kesha realized that although wanted to believe Kevin, there was still something amiss about the entire situation. Too many times she had seen other women get hurt by believing a dishonest man instead of looking at the facts. She slouched in her black leather chair with the tip of her pen in her mouth. It was a bad habit she had whenever she was in deep thought. She needed to think clearly; in fact, she needed the opinion of an outside party. Picking up the receiver, she dialled the extension number for the reception booth downstairs.

A woman with a clear professional voice picked up, giving her a warm greeting.

"Operator how I may direct your call?" the woman said without even realizing that it was her best friend Kesha on the line.

"Hey Mel, the calls are heavy this morning huh?" Kesha realized that the woman must have been trying to answer about a dozen calls at the same time, and did not even look at the number that was calling.

"Oh hey Kesha, what's up? Oh, hold on a minute," she said in a prompt sentence.

After what seemed like forever, Kesha heard her pick up the call again.

"Hey you there, I'm sorry about that, it's been a busy afternoon here. What's up love?"

Kesha carefully explained to her all what had transpired during the last few hours – the stranger coming to her office to accuse her of being a home wrecker, and confronting Kevin about it.

"What?" Mel shrieked in disbelief. "So what you do? You kicked Kevin out right?"

At that moment, Kesha felt a flash of embarrassment sweep across her face. She had definitely not kicked Kevin out. Instead, her stupid ass had gone over to his office furious and had left in joyful bliss. Kevin was a clever man, and the more she thought about it, the more she realized how he had once again manipulated her with sex.

"You did what now?" Mel had to catch her breath before she went on one of her rants with her. "Why you keep doing that Kesha? Stop letting that man use you, girl. You need to kick his tired ass to the curve, seriously. Kesha, you're my girl and all, so this is coming from the heart. This man doesn't respect you. He's always out. Who knows what he's doing, and he could very well be the father of this baby. Remember what happened to Marley and Rick? You don't want that to happen to you, trust me."

Kesha thought about what her friend had just said and realized, as much as she hated to admit it, Mel was right. Kevin was always doing suspicious stuff, and now that he was caught in a lie, he seemed to be manipulating her and getting away with it at that. She surely did not want to end up like Marley and Rick.

Marley was a co-worker who had been engaged to this guy Rick, or Sleek as the girls around the office had appropriately nicknamed him. Just days before their wedding, Rick took off to God-knows-where with his baby mama, leaving his fiancée Marley with thousands of dollars of debt on their house and all the wedding stuff that they'd already ordered. The whole situation sent Marley over the edge and finally she had a huge panic attack that led to her being institutionalized in a mental hospital for a few months. Since she'd gotten out no one had heard or seen her. The rumor was that she set out to find Rick for payback.

Kesha did not want any of that to happen to her. *Better end it now before anything like that happens*, she thought to herself. Mel was also ranting in her ear that she needed to get out of this bad relationship. Finally, she hastily ended the call. Everything Mel was saying was so true, and she could not bear another minute of the painful truth.

That evening when she got home Kesha knew exactly what she had to do. She picked up her phone to call Kevin, but as usual, he did not answer the call. By the third call, she realized that the phone had now been switched off because it went straight to his voicemail.

Yep, that's it. I'm done with this liar, she thought to herself as she searched through the closet and drawers, pulling out all of his stuff. She packed all of his belongings in a few garbage bags and threw them out on the front lawn. If he decided to come home before the garbage truck came by in the morning then he would get it. If not, oh well.

She closed the door and walked over to the wine cabinet, popping open a bottle of wine. That was the only thing that would help her get through this ordeal. "Ah, Sangria. How would I get by without you?" She gave the bottle of wine a soft kiss along its label. Normally wine would mellow her out and change whatever bad mood she was having.

She walked over to her fridge and pulled out a box of chocolates she had hidden way in the back. She almost felt guilty indulging in her favorite snack. *What the hell?* She thought. Kevin was not there to chastise her about it.

Kesha loved chocolate, but Kevin always discouraged her from eating too much of it. As she took another bite, she could hear Kevin's voice in her head telling her to throw it away; she'd had enough. But fortunately, that voice was but a soft minute voice in the back of her mind. She ate and ate, licking the chocolate off her fingers. How could anyone not love dark chocolate? That night when Kevin came home, he begged and pleaded with her, but she was not hearing any of it. A few glasses of red wine had made her wiser. As he tried to touch her, she found the strength to resist him. She threw him out, period. He looked shocked.

"You just need time to cool off," he said, making his way to his truck and speeding off into the night.

In the weeks that followed her breakup with Kevin, he made several attempts to get her back. "Just have lunch with me," he begged her on the phone. But she had grown weary of his lunches and his need to talk that somehow always led to sex and ended with her taking him back. This time the breakup was final – no talking, no meeting, nothing.

It had gotten so serious that one day while he was on the phone pleading with her to take him back, Mel snatched her phone and had a couple of very terse words for him, followed by a dramatic end where she called him "a no-good, lying, cheating, ugly ass motherfucker." She also made sure that she wished him nothing but hell with his so-called fiancée.

"That was not nice, Mel," Kesha told her. Although she was hurt by his actions, she did not want any harm or bad fortune to befall him. Somewhere deep down in her heart she still had a soft spot for him.

"What? Kesha! You need to move on and get over him already." There was a hint of irritation in Mel's voice as she tossed the phone back to her.

Kesha listened to see whether Kevin was

still on the call. Just like she suspected he'd ended the call. He was never one to tolerate any form of verbal abuse. She could do nothing but shake her head at her friend. Mel had always been the bold one between the two of them. She never sugarcoated her words. She would say exactly what she wanted to say to anyone who pissed her off. Many of the girls around the office really did not associate with her because of her sassy attitude. Kesha was just about the only good girlfriend that she had at work. In fact, Kesha was the only close friend she had, period.

She had been downstairs helping Mel with some paper work since it was Friday and they were both trying to leave work early before the heavy traffic. However, the paper work seemed endless. There were bits and pieces of various documents in several different draws in the filing cabinet. For someone who always had advice for others, Mel did not seem interested in hearing advice about getting more organized. Sorting out all of the paperwork that she had mixed all over her work area would probably take the entire day. Exasperated, Kesha finally gave up.

"C'mon let's go. You can do that on Monday," she encouraged as she got ready to leave.

"Yeah, I guess I can always catch up on Monday," Mel said, trying to tidy up her work area and lock all her drawers.

It was a little past nine in the evening and Kesha felt a cold wind of loneliness and boredom creeping up on her as she sat flipping through the channels trying to find something good to watch on TV. Finally, she found a somewhat interesting movie; however, just when she really started enjoying the story line, it came to an abrupt end. Irritated, she flipped to the TV guide channel to find out the movie had been on for the past hour and a half and it was truly at the end. She cursed under her breath, wishing that she had seen it from the beginning.

Her thoughts were interrupted by the sound of her mobile phone ringing. She frantically searched for it, first using her hand to search between the cushions and then finally getting up from her very comfortable couch to search the rest of the living room area. The phone stopped ringing before she found it, but it soon began ringing again. She stopped and listened attentively, finally narrowing down her search to back of her couch. There she found her phone vibrating and ringing at the same time.

The caller ID on her phone showed that it was Mel calling.

"Hi Mel, what's up?" she asked curiously. Mel seldom called her during the late hours of the night.

"Hey. I was just bored as hell, wondering if you wanted to go to the club or something. It is Friday night."

Kesha took a while to think about Mel's invitation; she had not been at a club in ages. She would not even know what to wear; much less know how to act when she got there. Besides, she was way too old to go clubbing.

Mel must have sensed her thoughts because she tried to convince Kesha to go with her. "C'mon Kesha, it's an adult club, just real grown folks. Who knows, you might even be able to hook up with someone there." She laughed at her comment.

"I'm not looking for any hook ups, Mel." This was probably the hundredth time she'd turned down Mel's attempts to get her a new man. It seemed like ever since her break-up Mel had made it her mission to find Kesha a new boyfriend. The list was endless; there was the Mr. Nice Ride, one of their clients that owned a set of very luxurious looking cars. There was a Mr. Coffee Shop, a handsome guy they had met in the coffee shop. Then there was Mr. Intern, which was by far the worst; she could not even tell whether he was twenty-two yet. His name was Michael and he was there at her office for an eight-week internship program. The entire time he was there Mel kept trying to hook them up.

"Don't front, Kesha. I'm sure you just as bored and lonely as me," she said, trying another tactic to change her mind.

Why did it seem like the people around her were always trying to manipulate her into doing things their way? Finally, Kesha gave in after enduring about half an hour of coaxing from Mel. She had about an hour to get ready for the club. She took a quick shower and opened the doors to her huge closet. She walked all the way to the back, flicking through the hangers. It had been a while since she went out and it would be difficult to find a suitable outfit. As she looked thoroughly at her closet, examining each one and then thinking of a reason why she could not wear it, her eyes caught wind of a shiny silver dress she had hidden way in the back. It seemed to call out to her. She strode to the back and pulled it off the rack. It was her birthday gift from Kevin from a couple years ago. *Will it still fit?* she wondered. It almost felt wrong wearing something he had bought her to go out clubbing now that they were no longer a couple.

Surprisingly the dress fit perfectly, accentuating all her curves in all the right places. "Wow," she said as she took a spin around in front of the mirror in the corner of her room. The next tough decision was her shoes.

Kesha was a shoe fanatic. She literally had hundreds of shoes in her closet; in fact, the entire left side of the closet was devoted to her shoe collection. Now that she needed to find a shoe to wear in a hurry, it seemed a bit ridiculous that she had all these shoes and never wore ninety present of them. Just as she did with the dresses, she picked each of her favorite ones up in one hand and examined them. Not realizing that the time was flying by, she sat on the stool in the closet and also tried them on one by one, visualizing how they would look in the club.

She had probably tried about sixty shoes when her phone rang again. It was Mel, of course. *She must be leaving her home now*, Kesha thought to herself. The two women had decided to car pool since Mel would have to drive past Kesha's house to get to the club.

In a nervous crackly voice, Kesha lied and told Mel that she was ready and was actually waiting for her outside. "Oh great, I thought I'd have to wait for you. I'm just swinging around the corner to your home now."

Kesha's gasped; she'd been caught in a lie. For the first time, she decided to lie to someone close to her, she was caught red-handed. "Um, Mel..." she said in a slow teasing voice.

"What? Where you at? I'm outside I can't see you?"

"Yeah... About that. Can you give me about ten to fifteen more minutes? I'll be out soon. I promise." She abruptly ended the call.

It took her well over fifteen minutes to get ready and when she got outside Mel had dozed off in her car. She tapped lightly on the glass on the driver's side, waking her up. The entire way to the club Mel ranted and raved about how she spent over an hour waiting in the car and had she not sincerely wanted to go out she would have driven off. Kesha ignored her. Over the years, Kesha had developed a unique skill of tuning people out. She would sit there and look interested, but in fact, her mind would be on a tropical island somewhere with one of her favorite actors, James Strong.

Soon they arrived at the club. Kesha was pleased to see the place was filled with grown mature people who seemed to be around her age. The music was great; it was more of an upscale bar than a club. She recognized the faces of a few clients that her firm had done business with in the past. Her attention also caught another familiar face, Devon Rod. Kesha and Devon had had a little fling during college but they never got past a few dinners and a few kisses. Devon had moved to another state to be with his ailing mom. She remembered him saying something about cancer. Her curiosity got the best of her, and as she walked over to where he had been standing with a drink in his hand, she wondered how he would respond to seeing her. More importantly, would he even remember who she was?

Devon looked strikingly handsome. He was just the type of man she had always dreamed of being with. His smooth dark chocolate complexion made her just want to savor his body. Apart from his gorgeous complexion, he had an amazing smile, perfect white teeth and a dimpled chin that gave him a smile to die for. And his body was simply divine, lean and athletic. She imagined that he could easily scoop her up in his arms. Devon Rod was a real man.

Kesha was elated to see that he remembered her. "I thought you wouldn't remember me."

"Forget you, impossible. I would never forget my college crush," he said, giving her a warm smile.

"Your crush? Wow, I'm flattered," she said moving closer to him.

He invited her to have a seat at a nearby table. They were soon joined by Mel, who had been in the ladies room. Kesha introduced the two of them and the three began ordering drinks. Halfway through the evening, the music changed and the lights were dimmed. "I guess it's that time," Devon teased.

Kesha looked puzzled - unlike Devon, this was her first time at the club. He explained to the two women that at midnight the bar would change into a club.

"Oh," Kesha gasped. That explained why when they arrived everyone was either seated at their tables or at the bar or just walking around. No one had been dancing.

A guy that had been eyeing them for a while walked over and invited Mel to dance with him. Kesha watched as Mel sprang to her feet and quickly made her way to the dance floor with this stranger.

"How about you, you think you still got it?" Devon had stood up and had his hand extended out to her. Had it been any other person, Kesha would have turned them down. But she found it hard to say no to Devon and his big hazel eyes that looked down into her very soul.

"Sure."

He led her to the dance floor and soon found a good spot in a corner. With his back against the wall, he pulled Kesha closer to him. Her back was now facing his front and she could feel his hot breath on her neck. She tried to focus on the beat of the music and move her hips in time, but it was hard with Devon standing right there behind her. She found herself very self-conscious. This was a man that she was extremely attracted to and he was less than an inch away from her.

"Let me get you a drink, it'll help you loosen up a bit," he whispered in her ears as he left her momentarily and headed in the direction of the bar.

He returned promptly with a drink in each hand. "Thanks," she said as brought up the drink to her mouth and took a few sips. Again, she brought it her lips and this time took a huge gulp. Hopefully drinking it like that would help her loosen up faster than if she were too slowly sip on it. He had returned to his position behind her and she could now feel him slowly grinding his body against her bum. The DJ was now playing one of her favorite R&B songs.

"Oh, hell yeah. That's my jam," she said with excitement in her voice. He looked pleased that she was now feeling the music and expressing herself freely. He gripped her waist and continued to move his body against hers. The moment was mesmerizing for Kesha and she was finally moving to the beat of the music. He'd been right; the drink did loosen her up. As she swayed her hips from left to right, she felt something hard press against her bum. She tensed up and stopped moving.

"Don't worry. It's just me. You don't have to stop," he whispered with a hoarse voice in her ear.

She could feel his warmness on her skin and as they continued to move, Kesha slowly began to feel her arousal. After a while, she could feel her saturated panties brushing against her pussy as she moved her hips to the music. His hand had cupped her waist, bracing her against his groin as he began to jerk his pelvis forward. Was he... was he humping her? Kesha shook her head in amazement. In the past, she had just thought it totally inappropriate to hump your body against a total stranger in a club, but now, with Devon it felt like the right thing to do. She began giving her hips small circular motions against his groin. She could feel the hard bulge almost piercing through the crotch of his pants. He was hard, and she was happy, very happy. *Maybe I would get laid tonight*, she thought with a smile.

Another song with a faster beat was now playing; he increased his moment and was now literally banging his body against hers. It was like sex with her clothes on. Her juices were flowing freely and she had never felt anything this intense without anybody being naked. They had not kissed, they had not licked, and they had not sucked or fucked. Yet here she was wet and horny. The more their bodies moved with each other the more aroused they both became. Soon his lips were caressing her earlobes. She moaned, a soft low moan, not wanting the couple a few inches away from her to hear. He stroked along her ear and then suddenly plunged his hot wet tongue inside her ear. She almost gasped out from the sudden gesture. Never in her life had anyone done anything wildly erotic to her in a public place. His tongue left her ears and was now stroking her gorgeous long neck.

His hand was also making their way

upwards and between her thighs. When he made contact with her moist flesh, a little groan escaped his lips. He was shocked to see how wet she was. As Kesha closed her eyes and moved to the beat of the music, Devon's hands probed the insides of her hot moist pussy. He took a few steps to his right, leading her into a darker corner where people could hardly see them. Once there he his lips came crashing down on the flesh sucking and licking the nape of her neck.

"My God, I want you so bad Kesha," he said in a hoarse voice that had an intense urgency in it.

She did not reply, she simply turned around facing him and locked lips with him in a deep passionate kiss. As they kissed, Kesha felt another hand, tapping lightly on her shoulder. She quickly broke away from his kiss and looked behind her.

A tall dark eyed man dressed all in black stood next to her. She could barely make out his face, but she did manage to hear his stern warning.

"This is a club, not a brothel," he said as ordered the two of them to leave the dark corner where they'd been standing. Kesha had never felt so embarrassed in her life; she buried her face in Devon's huge masculine chest.

Minutes later, she felt her phone vibrating in the small clutch she'd been carrying with her the entire night. It was a text from Mel.

"Hey girl, guess what? I'm in Mr. Hottie's apartment right now. Sorry for abandoning you but you look like you're in great hands. Hope

you get laid tonight, cuz I'm sure you're gonna get laid. XOXO"

A wave of anger swept through her. Mel had been her ride back home. How could she get so careless and just leave without even saying goodbye? She was about to text her back when the felt Devon's tongue back on her neck.

"Don't worry, no kissing, just a little teasing," he whispered in her ear, giving her earlobe a lingered lick.

She decided against texting Mel. Maybe this would all turn out for the best. Besides with Mel gone, if she got the opportunity to go home with Devon, she could just do it without feeling bad about it. Devon continued sucking on her neck while his hand lingered under her dress, his long fingers stroking the insides of her wet pussy. Soon the bouncer was back. This time he had much more firmness in his voice. He not only asked them to stop what they were doing, he asked them to leave the club and escorted them out himself. Praise God the people around were too busy dancing and focusing on their partners to realize what had happened. Devon looked unaffected by what was going on, but Kesha could not hide the look of embarrassment that now settled in on her face. How childish of her? No, how childish of the both of them? She did not know any people in their thirties who getting kicked out of clubs for public displays of affection. They were acting like teenagers all over again.

"So what now?" he asked, looking directly into her gray eyes. They were standing outside the club. At that moment, she wished for once in her life she could be just as bold as Mel. Had it been Mel in that situation, she would have probably made a big deal of the bouncer and then when she got outside she would have probably been all over Devon kissing him and making attempts to go to his home. But not Kesha. She was a calmer, timid woman.

Oh, what the hell, she thought to herself as she wrapped her arms around his neck and pulled him in for a kiss. As their lips met he groaned, his voice was cracked and she could hear the hunger in it. Her lips teased his, slowly biting on his bottom lip. His tongue went wild over hers as he pulled her in closer to him. She could feel the thudding of his heart. Over and over, their tongues lavished each other. Soon he was pushing her up against the wall on the side of the club. His hands were working their way up beneath her dress to the core of her womanhood. She moaned as she felt his hand stroke her wetness.

He gently used his fingers to massage her clit, rubbing against it hard at first then increasing his momentum. She let out another soft moan, as she moved her body perfectly against his strokes. Kesha decided to exchange the pleasure that he had released upon her. Her tongue was now along the nape of his neck, stroking it gently. His body tensed up a little as she heard him groan out in ecstasy. “Get a room!” they heard somebody from the distant shout. They both froze and they realized that they had been so hungry for each other that they had been almost fucking each other right outside of the club where anyone could see them. Although she hated to admit it, the passerby was right – they needed to get a room and they needed to get it as soon as possible.

Kesha figured the smart thing to do would be to go to her house. Whatever they would be doing tonight, she did not want to be the one who would have to wake up in the morning and head home.

“I live about ten minutes from here” she suggested. “We can go there, if you don’t mind.” She shocked even her own self with her bold move.

“Sounds like a great idea.” A look of excitement shot across his handsome face. Since she did not have her car, he had to drive the two of them. The distance to her home seemed further than it had been on her way there. Her heart was thudding in anticipation of what would come once they got to her home.

They could not keep their hands off each other once they arrived in the comfort of her home. His hand easily manipulated her body with its gentle caresses. Kesha moaned at the feel of his hand over her boobs. He was fondling them through her dress. As their kiss intensified, she longed to feel his wet hot tongue on her hardened nipples. Her moans must have conveyed her thoughts to him because he suddenly relieved her of the restriction of her apparel. Slowly her dress dropped to the floor, leaving her breast free for his tongue. She had not been wearing any bra, just her black thong. She had to catch her breath when she felt his palm make contact with her ass. He had given her a hard smack on her almost naked ass. His tongue left her mouth where it had been and trailed downwards to her nipples. With one gulp, he took almost half her breast in his mouth. His tongue stroked it over and over, as his hand gave her a gentle spanking on her ass cheeks.

"I want you now," he said breathlessly, leaning her over the couch in a swift movement.

Her ass was now popped out facing him. She jerked forward a little from the shock of feeling his tongue probing her pussy from behind. He had his face buried in her ass as his tongue teased along her slit. Kesha moaned, unable to control herself. In the past, she'd had guys suck her pussy, but none of them had ever bent her over and sucked her from behind. It felt amazing; there she was anticipating his dick being thrust inside her only to feel his hot wet tongue on her flesh.

He lavished the insides of her cunt from the back, occasionally thrusting his tongue inside her core. She especially enjoyed how he seemed to really enjoy doing it. He was rubbing his face between her ass cheeks. His tongue left her pussy and he glided it to her anus. She moaned in pleasure as he flicked his tongue over her asshole. Then she felt the tip of his tongue thrusting into her anus.

"Oh God," she moaned as he gripped the cheeks with both hands and his tongue went wild inside her anus. Thrusting it in and then flicking in and out of the hole. She clung to the armrest of the couch as he pleasured her from the back with his wickedly delicious tongue. Then she felt nothing; he had pulled his tongue away from her body. She turned around to see what he was doing.

Kesha mouth dropped and her eyes popped open at the sight of his erection. He had a huge dick – no, it was bigger than huge, it was humongous. It looked like a monster cock. As he stroked it, her eyes carefully examined it inch by inch. It had a dark brown tone to it, with huge bulging veins running across it from the base of his dick to its rim. It had a big purplish head that seemed equally proportioned to the rest of his cock. His entire length seemed slightly bent. At that moment as she admired his size, she felt a deep yearning to taste his chocolate rod. She took hold of him and gently stroked his full length with her fingers before indulging in it with her tongue. He tasted sweet, so sweet.

Over and over, she licked along his hard dick, flicking her tongue at its head, giving it small circular motions around the edges. “Suck it hard,” he said with a hoarse voice. With that, she took hold of his cock with her hot mouth, giving it long hard sucks. He groaned out in delirium. His hand gripped firmly against the back of her head, guiding it down on his cock. She gave him a serious of long hard strokes, causing his knee to wobble as the ecstasy of it all ruptured his entire being. She increased her momentum, sucking on his dick with more vigor. As she took him in and out her mouth, she found herself getting more and more aroused. Her juices were flowing like a waterfall. The desire to fuck him was so intense that she left his dick and led him to her huge sofa.

She lay on her back with her legs spread open waiting for him to mount her. He swiftly made his way over to her and plummeted his dick inside her with great force. She shrieked in pain as her fingers clawed at the sofa. Her pussy was hot and wet and it made him let out a long deep groan. His full dick inside her pussy sent shockwaves through her entire body. He increased his momentum, fucking her even harder than before. Their bodies move in perfect rhythm as their moans filled the room.

Kesha could feel her cum approaching. She gripped firmly into the cushions and closed her eyes. Letting out a loud moan, she peaked her climax. Her body shivered as he continued to ram her pussy with his still very erect cock. He seemed like a fully charged Energizer bunny. The wetness of her pussy seemed to motivate him even more. His thrusts were now hard and quick. He was panting with each thrust. Suddenly he increased his momentum he was now fucking her harder than she'd ever been fucked in her life. Her breasts bounced viciously back and forth as he banged her. Finally, with a long stretched out groan he released his load of hot cum inside her wet pussy. She looked up at him and could see the sweat glistening on his chocolate brown skin.

They sat up before slouching back onto the couch. "That was amazing," he said. He maintained an intense look on his face, as the tiny smile that he had on his face broadened, exposing a row of perfect white teeth.

"Yeah it was," she agreed, laying her head on his shoulder.

They were about to fall asleep on the couch when he decided to leave. She wanted to ask him to stay, but she decided against it. After getting dressed, she walked him to the door and there they shared another passionate kiss that left them both lightheaded. She could not get enough of him. He was like rich dark chocolate; she could never get enough of it.

Several months had gone by since Kesha had reconnected with Devon at the club. They had been spending more time together. Kesha was "taking things slow" with this new relationship. She had vowed that she would never let another man hurt her way Kevin had. Devon seemed to be a good guy though; he was pretty much an open book with her. They would spend hours talking about their past, their goals and their future. The more they spent time together the more she slowly began removing the wall that she had put up. Her relationship with Devon was the complete opposite of her relationship with Kevin. She was the center of his world; nothing else mattered but her. Career-wise, he had a good job at a marketing company, and she appreciated that it was a basic nine-to-five job; there was no overtime, no, "I have to work twice as hard since I'm my own boss."

Although their relationship was still young,

when they'd been together just over six months Kesha found herself envisioning what it would feel like to be Mrs. Kesha Rod. Yes, that sounded just right.

Today was his birthday and she had decided to cook him something. As she stood in the line at the grocery store, she could not help but have doubts about her plans for the evening. Was she kidding herself? She was definitely not a homemaker and cooking was not her forte. In the past on special occasions, she would just take the birthday boy out to dinner somewhere. However, there was something different about this relationship; she wanted it to work more than ever.

She wanted to be more hands-on, thinking that maybe if she'd been cooking and doing more around the house, Kevin would have proposed to her. A rush of anger shot through her at the thought of Kevin and his estranged so-called fiancée. For a minute, she wondered how he was doing. Had he gotten everything she could not give him from this other woman?

"Next!" a stout woman at the cash registered said in a loud voice that caught her attention.

Kesha took a few steps forward and pulled out her credit card, awaiting the total of her groceries, her eyes fixed to the cashier's computer screen. She had always double-checked what the cashier was doing. In the past, she caught cashiers accidentally duplicating item codes and overcharging her. This had made her all the more wary of them. She knew that they'd probably just been tired from a long shift. After all, everyone had moments when exhaustion would get the best of them.

"Sixty-two fifty," the woman said lifting her gaze from her computer screen to Kesha.

"Damn," Kesha muttered under her breath. She could have gone to eat out and spent just about the same thing, minus the manual labor involved in cooking the food. All she'd bought was some pork chops, soft cornbread mix, chocolate syrup, strawberries... As she watched the woman bag her groceries, the doubt she had about the total cost of her items faded. As much as she hated admitting it to herself, she did have quite a lot of stuff. The woman's expression betrayed a little annoyance as she waited anxiously for Kesha to swipe her credit card. With no more hesitation Kesha swiped the blue card and used the pen attached the small device to do her digital signature. As she left the store, her anticipation heightened. Where would she begin with all the preparations?

It was about fifteen minutes into her cooking when the alarm on the oven went off, signalling that her cornbread was ready. Originally, she had planned to bake the pork chops, but since she had spent so much time at the grocery store, she decided to just do some fried pork chops, cornbread and green beans. It wasn't much, but at least he would see that she had put a little effort into it. As she heard his car pull up in the driveway, Kesha dropped everything and run upstairs to take a quick shower and put on the sexy lingerie she'd bought especially for tonight.

Her steps were slow and precise as she made her way back downstairs in the seven-inch heels she also bought special for that night. *Gosh, I look like a damn fool,* she thought to herself as she tried hard to catch herself from slipping over and falling. When she had seen the shoes in the store, she thought they would complement her lingerie, but now that she actually had to walk in them, they felt like a stupid idea.

All the fear and anxiety she had felt coming down the stairs subsided when she saw his reaction. His mouth dropped open and his eyes lit up. She could tell that he was impressed. "Wow, you really went all out baby," he said in a hoarse voice.

Swaying her hips from left to right, Kesha took a few steps toward him. Her heart thudded as she bit on her lower lip, her body yearning to be one with his. The intensity in his eyes was astounding and as the gap between them narrowed, she could feel her own arousal growing with every passing step.

They made it through dinner, but while they were physically full, emotionally they were still very hungry for each other. She was sipping on some red wine when he walked around the table to where she was sitting.

"Thanks for dinner. I really enjoyed it, love." He leaned in and planted a soft kiss on her forehead. That kiss ignited the flames of desires that had been simmering inside her from the beginning of the evening. She sprung up from her sea, and their lips met almost instantly. His lips were moist and hunger-filled. Their kiss was so intense that they had to pull away for a few seconds to catch their breath. Their tongues danced together in sweet ecstasy. Scooping her up in his arms, he went upstairs to her bedroom.

He gasped as he opened the door. The room was lit up with candles and the sweet aroma seemed to intoxicate them both. The bed was covered with rose petals; a box of chocolates served as the centerpiece in the sea of red. From the look on his face, she could tell that he was touched.

"Wow, no one's ever done all this for me," he said as his eyes surveyed the room, taking in the beautiful ambiance.

"Happy birthday, love."

It was probably the hundredth time she had said it that day.

"I just wanted to make sure your day was special."

She took a few steps closer to him and looked up at him. His eyes fell directly into hers and she almost melted. "Cause you're special to me, and you deserve nothing but the best," she continued. His lips met hers and they both lost themselves in a deep passionate kiss.

Kesha could feel tiny sensations making their way down from her mouth to her pussy. Their hands were now going wild over each other's bodies. His lips parted with hers making their way down the nape of her neck. He sucked her flesh hard, like he wanted to suck the life out of her. She moaned. Her eyes felt like they were rolling to the back of her head as she tilted her head back in pure ecstasy. He continued his powerful sucks while his hands stroked her almost bare flesh. She could feel juices slowly trickling down her pussy, saturating her panties.

When he stopped kissing her neck, she decided it was her turn to pleasure him. She slowly went down to her knees; her hand was quickly unbuckling the belt of his pants. His pants dropped to the floor; he was not wearing any underwear, just like Kesha had suspected.

She remembered asking him one day why he didn't wear underwear under his trousers. "I like going commando, baby," he had replied with a smirk on his face. Before that day, she had never met any guy like Devon. He was a free spirit and she admired the way he lived life not letting anything or anyone bother or change him. Kesha focused her attention on the task at hand, caressing his huge cock.

He had to catch his breath when she took him into her mouth. As her tongue stroked his full length, he groaned out begging her not to stop. She firmly gripped his dick with her mouth and moved her lips up and down on it, sucking it long and hard. The more she sucked the harder and longer it got. His dick was now almost double the size it had been when she first took it into her mouth.

"Kesha," he groaned his voice husky and full of desire.

She sucked on the dick harder when she heard the urgency in his voice. Working her tongue up to the head of his dick, she focused her attention on caressing it a bit. She flicked her tongue over it, giving it smaller, gentle sucks. He was barely able to stand still his knees were so shaky. She felt flattered that his body reacted with such intensity to the feel of her tongue. Again and again, she ravished his dick with her tongue; giving it a combination of long, hard sucks, slow, gentle licks and deep kisses. She finally released his dick and led him to the bed. She brushed the box of chocolates aside. She did not need artificial chocolate when she had the real deal in front of her.

She quickly got out of her bra and panties. As he lay there on his back, she mounted him. Her wet pussy going down on his dick felt amazing. A soft moan escaped her lips as she tried to get comfortable on his huge cock. It felt like it would literally rip her pussy apart with its massiveness. Taking a deep breath, she slowly began riding it. As she went up and down on his dick, her full, melon-shaped breasts bounced up and down. It must have tantalized him because after a while he leaned up and took them in his mouth. A quick jolt of pleasure rushed through her body when she felt his hot wet tongue caressing her nipple.

"Ahhh," she moaned as she closed her eyes and bucked her pussy hard against his dick. Her juices were oozing out of her pussy and onto his raw meat. Up and down she went on his hard, erect dick, moaning loudly in sweet ecstasy. Her bare skin glistened from the sweat that resulted from her rapid movements.

His hand was now on her hips guiding her pussy downwards. As their passion increased so did the momentum of their movements. Devon was now heaving his body off the bed meeting her pussy half way, given her several hard upwards thrusts. Their bodies moved in sweet harmony, their thrusts corresponding perfectly.

Devon increased his thrusts as his grip on her hips tightened. He had a dark look in his eyes. He was about to cum. With a series of mighty quick upwards thrusts his cum shot up inside her pussy. A loud moan escaped her lips as she too released and reached an earth-shattering climax.

Exhausted she fell to his side and tried to catch her breath. That night they slept in each other's arms and Kesha found herself enjoying a dream where the two of them were married and living happily with two kids.

Kesha sat at her desk, busy shopping online instead of getting ready for her next case. Suddenly her door swung open and, lo' and behold, Kevin walked in waving a piece of paper in his hand.

Her secretary rushed in after him. "I tried to stop him from entering Miss Whitfield," she said frantically.

"It's okay," Kesha said, waving her hand at the young woman, who left the two of them.

"I told you," he said in a firm thunderous voice extending out the piece of paper he had in his hands. "It's the paternity test. When the baby looked nothing like me, I knew I was right from the start. This proves what I was trying to tell you all alone. I am not the father of Gale's baby."

Kesha could not believe her ears. She was speechless. Had he provided her with that information a few months ago she could probably take him back, but now she was with Devon. And she was happy with him. The past few months with him were the happiest months of her life. Although she still had some love for Kevin, she could not just forget about Devon and get back with him.

"I'm sorry but I still can't be with you," her voice was sad and mellow. She could hardly look him straight in the face.

"But why? I am here with the evidence that proves that I am not this child's father. I told you Gale was a mistake; it only happened one time. I swear!" He moved in closer to her. His body was hot against hers, "Please baby, I need you. I can't be without you. I'm sorry for everything that I did. I'm desperate. I need you and only you," he begged.

It broke her heart to see him plead with her. There was a deep yearning in his eyes and she could hear the pain in his voice. *Perhaps he was truly sorry. Maybe he has changed,* she thought to herself.

"I don't know Kevin...." Suddenly his lips were on hers, hungry and desire-filled. His skin was hot and his scent was familiar. All the feelings that she had spent months trying to get over were now awakening with a vengeance. She found herself returning to her former state of complete weakness to his touch. Her body ached for more as his tongue caressed her tongue. Their tongues went wild for each other. She could tell that her body had missed his tender touch.

At that moment, she forgot about everything that had happened and immersed herself in the passion of his kisses. His mouth left hers and found her neck. He stroked the length of her neck while his hand fondled her breasts through her blouse. She moaned out in ecstasy. He hurriedly popped the buttons of her blouse, exposing her semi-naked flesh. *Thank God I had worn a new black lace bra this morning*, she thought. Their kisses grew more intense and soon she felt her bra become loose and watched as it dropped to the floor. Her breasts sprang free.

His mouth caught one of her nipples and he pleasured her thoroughly. She thought she would lose her mind as his tongue flicked viciously against her hard nipples. She moaned out with ecstasy as he braced her up against the wall of her office. He left her momentarily and headed over to the door. He locked it securely and pulled down the blinds before making his way back to where she'd been standing with her back against the wall.

His kisses on her nipples became gentler and she found herself wishing that he would suck them harder. She surprised herself when she moaned out and asked him to fuck her now.

He did not hesitate, immediately unzipping her skirt and dropping it to the floor as he ripped her panties off. She almost gasped in disbelief as his dick made its appearance. It looked bigger than she remembered. Kesha could not tell whether her mind was playing tricks on her, or whether he'd grown a few inches.

"You're huge" her voice weak with desire.

"Thank you, but I think I'm just happy to see you," he said with a wicked little smile on his face.

They moved in closer to each other and this time when their mouths met, their bodies quivered from the intensity of their desires. His hand roamed all over her naked body, making a stop at her hot wet pussy. As he slipped one finger inside her, a soft moan escaped her lips. She threw her head back in delirium. He stroked her tender flesh over and over with his finger. He worked his way up to her throbbing clit, gently teasing it with his index finger. Another moan and she closed her eyes. Her body had always been very receptive to his caresses. How was he able to do that even after months of not seeing or talking to him?

He pulled his finger out of her moist center and stroked his long hard dick a few times. Using his hands, he hoisted one leg to his side and positioned himself between her hoisted leg and her leg that held up in standing position. He groaned as his dick made contact with her pussy the first time in almost a year. She took a deep breath as he penetrated her insides, further bracing her up against the wall. When his full length had made its way up her cunt, he groaned again, and pulled out instantly only to penetrate her again with more force. She gripped his shoulders as he tightened the grip he had on her elevated leg and gave her several hard thrusts. Her moaning grew louder and louder. His lips came crashing down on hers muffling the loud moans that would probably have her co-workers knocking at the door in suspicion. Over and over, he gave her several hard thrusts that had her crying out for more.

Finally with a mighty thrust he exploded his juices inside of her. Her body quivered from her own climax that she had around the same time as his. Just as he was pulling his dick out of her pussy, the phone rang. She swiftly made her way to the phone, taking a deep breath before picking up the receiver.

"Are you guys fucking in there?" Mel voice sounded like she was highly irritated.

The question caught Kesha off guard and she took a few minutes trying to think of a good answer.

"What are you talking about Mel?' she asked, twisting the cord around her index finger as she anxiously waited to hear what Mel had to say.

"I just got a call from one of my sources upstairs and apparently they heard moaning sounds coming out of your office."

"Moaning sounds?" she asked trying to joke about it to cut the tension.

"Yeah bitch, moaning sounds. Don't play stupid. Anyway, I hope you didn't just fuck that jerk. That's all I'm saying." Mel's voice was cold and emotionless.

Kesha looked over to where Kevin was getting dressed; he was just about to put on his polo shirt.

"Listen, Mel, I don't know what they heard but nothing's going on in here," she tried to reassure the woman at the other end of the line.

"Well good, because I just saw Devon a couple of minutes ago taking the elevator up."

"What are you...?" Their conversation was interrupted by the knocking at the door.

She did not even realize what Mel was trying to tell her.

"Who is it?" she called out, motioning Kevin to hide in the small bathroom in her office.

"It's me." Devon's voice sounded from behind the door.

Kesha's heart raced. Of all the times when Devon could show up at her office, why did he have to pick now?

Mel must have heard what was going on because she quickly informed Kesha that she was on her way. She was never one to miss out on some good drama.

"I'll be right there," Kesha replied, hanging up the receiver and walking over to the bathroom door behind which Kevin was hiding.

"Don't come out until I tell you too," she warned as she made her way to the other door to let Devon in.

Devon looked incredibly handsome. He wore a navy blue top with khaki shorts and still managed to look his best. Kesha had to admit he was just a charmer. As he walked in, he pulled her into his arms and planted a soft kiss on her lips. Kesha had never felt so uncomfortable in her life. What if he could tell that she'd just been kissing another man? She pulled away from his kiss out of disgust for herself.

"I was just wondering whether you wanted to get some lunch or something?" he asked as he held her in his arms.

Any other day she would have happily picked up her bag and left, perhaps even for the rest of the day. Her lunch dates with Devon often led back to her home or his apartment. She did not want to risk going on a lunch date and ending up at having sex with him only minutes after she'd had sex with Kevin. Just thinking about that made her stomach turn a little. She would be an absolute slut if she did that.

There was another knock at the door.

"Who is it?"

"It's Mel." The door swung open as Mel made her way inside with curious eyes.

Her eyes carefully examined every inch of the room as if she were searching for some hidden treasure.

"Yes, how can I help you Mel?" Kesha asked, startling her a bit and causing her to focus her attention on Kesha and Devon.

"Um, well, I just came to borrow your stapler," she said, walking over to the large mahogany desk and picking up the stapler that sat close to the edge.

Devon greeted Mel and, of course, she asked him what he was doing around the office. He was polite and never got offended by her somewhat intruding questions. He told her that he'd just come to take Kesha for lunch.

"Oh really, lunch you say? Have you had

anything to eat yet Kesha?" she asked with a hint of sarcasm in her voice.

"No," Kesha shot back at her, irritated at the fact that her friend would insinuate anything like that in front of her boyfriend.

"You know what, I was busy but I would love to go out to lunch with you," Kesha said with a little arrogance in her voice. "Let me tidy up here a few minutes and I'll be right out. You can wait for me in the car and I'll be right down," she said to Devon.

"Okay, great," he replied as he said goodbye to Mel and left, closing the door behind him.

As soon as the door closed, Kevin sprang out of the bathroom.

Mel gasped in disbelief. A part of her knew Kevin was probably there, but she was secretly hoping that he'd already left.

"Kevin!" she shrieked, her eyes moving from Kesha to him and then back to Kesha. "What's going on here?" she asked in a tone of voice that almost made it seem like she was Kesha's mom and had just busted them.

Kevin replied first. "What's going on is that I love this woman," he said, pointing to Kesha. "And I want to be with her." He dropped down on one knee and pulled out a small black box.

Kesha gasped as her hands covered her lips in shock. "What are you doing, Kevin?" she asked.

Mel stood there speechless, not knowing what to say or do. She did not like Kevin; in her heart, she could feel some deep negative energy coming from him. She had always been able to read into certain men, those that had secrets, who cheated on their girlfriends.

Although Mel wanted to say "No, don't say yes," this had to be a decision Kesha made on her own, without anybody else interfering.

Mel looked on with curious eyes hoping that her friend would say no to this his proposal.

Kesha looked at the exquisite diamond pensively before responding. She did have feelings for Kevin and they had been ignited by their moment of passion in her office.

"Kesha, please say yes. I want it all with you – the baby, the house, family. I want these things with you girl."

It sounded like he was pleading with her to take the ring.

Kesha thought for a minute. She was in love with Devon. She remembered all the times that they had spent together. She could not just forget about Devon. She would be hurting him when he had been nothing but nice to him. Kevin, on the other hand... Yes, he had proved he was not the father of Gale's baby, but he had still admitted to cheating on her. Like her mom always told her, "Once a cheater, always a cheater."

Kesha knew exactly what she had to do. "I'm sorry Kevin, I can't. We have been through too much. I just can't deal with that again."

"It's the new guy isn't it?" he asked with a look of concern on his face.

Although Devon was part of the reason why she did not want to be with Kevin, all of their past problems weighed heavily on her heart. All the late night calls, the times when he would not come home at all. No, she could not put off by any of that. Her relationship with Devon was perfect and she did not want to jeopardize it.

"It's everything, Kevin. I can't be with you. You need to move on. We're done," she finally said to him.

There were mixed feelings in the room. Kevin looked crushed and heartbroken, while Mel looked happy. She was proud of Kesha's decision.

Kevin slowly closed the box and put the ring back in his pocket. "I wanted to give you everything," he said to her coldly.

"It's too late now, Kevin," she said to him, walking over to the door to see him out. He left her office with his head bent in shame.

As soon as he left, Mel rushed off to where she was standing.

"That's my girl!" she said, giving Kesha a high-five.

"I wished he would have done all this a few months ago, before I met Devon. But it's too late right now. I am in love with Devon now."

"Ahh, Devon," Mel teased, taking in a deep breath.

"I know, right. Isn't he drop-dead gorgeous? Just thinking about him gives me the shivers." Kesha laughed out loud.

"He mighty fine, isn't he?" Mel said as they walked over to the window, looking down at the parking lot where Devon was seated in his convertible with the top dropped back.

"Yep, that's my handsome dark chocolate Rod," Kesha teased as the two of them left the office. She looked forward to lunch with him

That day they had lunch and as they ate

Kesha knew with more certainty that she had made the right decision turning down Kevin's proposal. Devon Rod was definitely the man for her.

2 HIS PERSONAL SEXETARY

Laura Carter walked down the length of her hallway and entered her eloquently decorated bedroom to look at herself in the full length mirror one last time. She wondered for the hundredth time whether she was appropriately dressed for this morning's interview.

This was her tenth interview in just as many weeks, and she was anxious to make a good first impression. She had spent over an hour brushing her silky hair until it shone like jewels in the mid-morning sun. She had carefully selected her black jacket with a white colorless shirt and matching black skirt cut just above her knees showing off long beautiful dark legs. Laura had chosen a black pair of high heel sandals and a fashionable black handbag.

She smiled with satisfaction at herself. She looked okay. No, she looked better than okay, she looked amazing. She headed toward the front door. Would this interview be any different than the rest? She would be meeting with some well-off arrogant man who would ask her a million questions about her background, education, likes, dislikes, hobbies, and friends. In the end of the long drawn-out process, he would promise to call her if she were suitable for the job. But as usual she would go home, anxiously awaiting that call that she would never get.

She hoped this one would be different. She wanted this job. She had just graduated from college and had all the prerequisite qualifications for that job. She remembered the call had come at five thirty last evening. The voice was masculine with a deep cultured accent.

The message was brief and she was invited to attend an interview at eleven in the morning the following day.

"Here you are Miss," the taxi driver announced fifty minutes after she first boarded his car. Laura handed the mature-looking Chinese man his fare and carefully disembarked the yellow car. She focused on her every movement so as not to shuffle her outfit or her hair.

With a few strides she was at the front door of the huge building, with "Satin and Barnaul" written across the transparent glass front door in a bold white font. In the building Laura's eyes perused her environment as she walked up to the reception booth. An attractive redhead stood behind the booth with an earpiece mechanically answering the phone that seemed to ring endlessly. The woman was so busy that it took her a few minutes to even acknowledge Laura's presence.

"Just one moment, ma'am," the red-haired woman said, looking up briefly at Laura.

"How can I help you, ma'am?" she said after about five minutes.

"Hi, my name is Laura Carter. I have an interview here at eleven, and..."

She quickly placed a call to her boss informing him that he had a visitor.

As Laura stood there, she could feel her heartbeat increasing. Her nervousness was mounting with every passing second. She shifted uneasily in her chair. She picked the pendant of her gold chain and played with it impatiently, a habit that came to her whenever she was anxious or nervous.

"Follow me," she heard a calm voice say. Laura hoisted her head and realized that the slender red-haired woman was now several strides ahead of her. She quickly picked up her bag and followed her. The woman stopped abruptly and knocked on a huge brown door with a silver knob.

"Come in," a deep husky voice called out from behind the door. Laura's heart almost skipped a bit as she recognized the same voice from the night before. Could it be? Why would the manager of such a large, million dollar corporation be the one to call her for an interview? Laura was thoroughly confused. But she was able to maintain her composure throughout the interview. The interview had been very informal, and Mr. Satin asked her a few questions which had absolutely no significance to the position for which she had applied.

She went home that afternoon feeling worse than she had ever felt after any of her interviews. She knew she was awaiting a call that would never come. Yet she held up her hopes. The interview had gone... Well, not bad – minus all the useless questions – there were at least two or three good ones. She had done her research immediately after she'd received the invitation last evening, so she was well prepared for the few relevant questions.

When she arrived home she made herself a cup of tea, settled into the oversized lazy chair and made a call to her sister, Maryanne, who was also her best friend.

Maryanne was the first of her mother's two children. Being only two years older than her, Maryanne was always there for her, giving her sisterly advice in everything she did. So there she was calling her one more time telling her about the interview and asking her what she thought were her chances of landing that job. A good job, she felt – Executive Secretary to the CEO of a large corporate consulting firm. If she landed this job, it could mark the beginning of a brand new era for her and her family.

She was brought up in a low- to middle-class family in a nondescript area in the Bronx, New York. She knew that it took a lot of hard work to make it in this society, but she was determined to do all it took to succeed.

Several days later, Laura had completely forgotten about her last interview, when the telephone rang. She wondered who it might be as she walked to answer the extension on the kitchen wall.

"Hello?" she spoke into the mouthpiece. When the person answered on the other side of the line, she nearly fainted. Her heart skipped a beat. Chris Satin! It was unbelievable. He had called her back, really!

Mr. Satin informed her that she had been considered for a job that was one rank higher than the job she had applied for since that job had already been filled. He said he was offering her the job of Personnel Secretary. She would work alongside him. She would be given a company car and a higher monthly salary, would attend overseas meetings and conferences, and above all, would be given commissions and year-end bonuses. She was absolutely thrilled at the prospect. He requested that she report to work on Monday morning at 8:00 a.m. She thanked him profoundly and hung up the telephone.

The weekend passed by swiftly. On Saturday she shopped for new work clothes. She also rearranged her closet, cleaned her apartment, and restocked her refrigerator and cupboards.

On Monday morning she set out with high anticipation for her new job. She entered the office at seven thirty, giving herself sufficient time to settle down and relax a bit. She expected today being her first day on the job, she would be shown around, familiarize herself with the environment, and basically have an easy day.

Her expectations were gravely shattered

when the receptionist had led her to a small office exactly opposite Mr. Satin's massive one. Two minutes later Mr. Satin pushed his broad frame into the doorway and requested that she come into his office.

He laid a rumpled stack of papers before her. "Organize chronologically and file," he said curtly. He then handed her several handwritten file sheets of paper with names and addresses highlighted in red, yellow, and blue markers. "Set appointments in order of urgency, red has first priority, then blue, and finally yellow." She took the second stack of papers.

"Lunch is at one, meet me at the manager's reserved side of the parking lot. I know a great restaurant which serves a variety of exotic dishes. I usually go there to relax and get work done during my lunch break. It will be a great opportunity for you to change your environment and get some work done in the process." He had a slight smile on his face that seemed a bit confusing considering the fact that he was asking her to work during her lunch hour.

He exited the room briskly, and as Laura sat there trying to remember all what he had instructed her to do, she just wanted to scream out and release her frustration. She looked through her small door and could see him outside on his cell phone deep in conversation.

She had questions lingering in her mind, but she did not know how or when to ask them. He seemed like he was so, so busy. Taking in a deep long breath, she slowly began doing all the tasks that he had assigned to her. Soon her mind was blocked from all the distractions of her environment, and she buried herself into her work. When she finally stopped for a breather, she realized that time had escaped her and it was now a few minutes before lunch.

Putting down everything, she hurriedly made her way out of her minute office and headed outside to meet with Mr. Satin. As she stood outside her eyes caught wind of Mr. Satin exiting the front door to her left.

"Here you go, it's the black BMW in the third parking spot to your right," he said as he handed her a bunch of car keys. The entire time she had been thinking that he would be driving her to the restaurant but sadly it was the other way round. She was now his secretary and driver. How could this day get any worse? she thought to herself as she walked over to the luxurious-looking vehicle. At the restaurant a special table had been reserved for them, near a window which overlooked a playground. The table was elegantly set with a beautiful bouquet of flowers in the center of it. Laura looked around for a minute and realized that something was a little odd. Her table was the only table with flowers on it.

"They are for you," his voice was husky with pleasantness in it that she had not heard. He handed her the bouquet of flowers.

"Thank you, sir," she said, trying to maintain her composure. Was he coming on to her? Why would he get her flowers? Laura had several unanswered questions lingering in her mind. She finally came to the conclusion that he was just being humble. Besides, even if he were coming on to her, that would not necessarily be a completely bad thing. He was a handsome successful business mogul. And it would be an honor, a privilege even, for her, a recently graduated student, to get his attention. Her thoughts were interrupted by the waitress, a slender blond woman.

Mr. Satin smiled at the young woman. She smiled back. "What you are having today, Chris?" she asked in a warm friendly voice. They obviously knew each other so much so that she was calling him by his first name. At that moment Laura felt a little bit of jealousy, and she wished she were the one being that friendly with him; she wished she could call him "Chris,"

The woman handed them both their menus and said she would be back to get their orders. Laura watched as she strode across the room to another table, going through basically the same procedure she had done with them. Her smile, which had seemed so genuine, looked very unauthentic at that moment. Soon she was back at their table to take their order.

Laura ordered a baked potato, chicken stew in sour sauce, peas, and a large portion of steamed vegetables. While Mr. Satin simply said that he would have the regular meal that he always has. The waitress walked away with their order writing down on the small notepad she had in the palm of her hands. About ten minutes later, she was back bearing their various dishes.

As she ate Laura noticed that Mr. Satin had brushed her hand twice for no apparent reason. She looked at him across the rim of her water glass. His eyes were bright and filled with desire, although his demeanor was distant and reserved. He brushed his hands against hers another time as he reached over to get the basket of rolls. She could hardly control herself at the feeling of his touch upon her flesh. A tangy stream of pleasure ran down the back of her spine and crashed down between her thighs. Laura chastised herself for her stupidity; she was acting like a silly teenager. She decided to try to focus on the meal in front her.

Laura thoroughly enjoyed her meal to the last bite. She washed down the food with a glass of orange juice and a glass of water. The entire time her boss did not mention work once; instead, she saw a softer, more compassionate side to him. He laughed at her jokes and occasionally told her jokes of his own. Had he not been so uptight she would have thought that it was a date. Finally, after they were done with lunch, he handed his credit card to the waitress who had handed them the bill.

That day was actually the first time they really just released and enjoyed each other's company. When they got back from lunch, Mr. Satin was the perfect gentleman; he opened the front door to let her into the building before him, and he even dropped her off in her office. At the door to her office, he stopped and surprisingly gave a soft peck on the forehead, saying that he had enjoyed lunch with her.

Laura quivered and she would have fallen had she not quickly leaned against the door frame of the small office.

In his office, Mr. Satin reflected upon the events of the day. He knew that his feelings for Laura were very inappropriate. He cursed himself silently for allowing his dick to control his actions. Had it been any other ordinary woman, he would not have even hired them, but here he was taking his personal secretary to lunch. Talking about, "they serve a variety of exotic dishes." How could he have been so dumbstruck by such a naïve-looking young woman. He had been attracted to her from day one, when she attended the interview. He had known from that point that he would have to exercise restraint given the fact that he had only recently split up with his wife. And although she had run off with another much younger man, he had not quite given up on her or their relationship. She had been his high school crush and the love of his life.

For a moment Mr. Satin sat back in his big comfortable leather chair and wondered what his wife was doing. Was she truly happy? Did she find what she had been looking for in this younger guy?

He managed to finally pull himself out of a pit of questions and comforted himself by thinking that she had always been a little too hot-headed for him. So in one way, her leaving gave him a sense of freedom that he had not had for a while now. Deep down inside Mr. Satin knew that he had to let her go. She had treated him badly enough at it was, embracing him with her malicious actions. He had always wanted her to bear him a child which she had never done, stating that the time was not right, but as the years had gone by, it had seemed like that would never be a right time. He had known the reason for her resistance, but he had kept silent about it. She genuinely did not want to spoil her slender well-shaped body.

She always felt that with an oversized tummy and swollen breasts she could not return to her normal size. But everyone else did, and so he wondered what planet she lived on. He knew she was not in the business of making babies, but she hid under the disguise of poor timing. He had loved his wife and they had several good years of marital bliss. She too had promised to love him, but when the time came to prove it by setting everything else aside and becoming parents, she almost had a stroke at the thought of becoming pregnant. He would always be forced to drop the issue to get her to relax.

However, all the love and luxuries in the world could not prevent her from walking away from their relationship. Mr. Satin lost himself in the memory of how she had left him. They had not had an argument or a fight; in fact, he had thought that it was all good between them. Until he came to an empty condo. There on the coffee table sat a note, at the time he had thought it was just a gentle reminder that she had for him about something that he needed to do. He remembers everything she had put in her little note from him.

Dear Chris,

I am sorry it has come to this, but I can't anymore. I don't want to be living this lie anymore. I want someone who is not so consumed with their job. We had some good times, and I wish you the best in all your future endeavors. Please don't try to contact me and make this any harder than it already is. I met someone. He is 24 but very mature. He is totally devoted to me and I'm the center of his universe. I am sorry. I hope that you too can one day find someone else and move on.

Love Always, Amy

P.S. I already called my lawyer and she will send you the divorce papers. I don't want anything much, just one of the cars and some money to get on my feet again.

He had almost had a heart attack after reading her note. How could she have been so cruel toward him? After everything that they had been through together, she was perfectly fine with just leaving him and serving him with some divorce papers, blaming everything on the fact that he was a hard worker. What was he supposed to do? Until now thoughts of another woman head not even crossed his mind. Laura had something about her that made it seem like she was worth the while. He could not quite put his finger on it, but there was something about her that made his head spin and his heart thud. Thoughts of her naked in his arms, begging him to make love to her consumed his entire being. He wanted to touch her, kiss her, and even make love to her. She was an attractive intelligent young woman with this hidden passion in her eyes.

He had seen it from the minute she first

walked through his door, the look of a woman yearning to be released, to experience ecstasy like never before. In the past he had had one office relationship with one of his colleagues. It had ended abruptly when she transferred to another state and left him to pick up the pieces. That was when he met Amy. She was a breath of fresh air, older than most of the girls that he had dated, and her maturity seemed to draw him closer and closer to her.

Mr. Satin jumped out of his deep moment of thought at the sound of the sudden knock at the door. "Are you alright?" Laura asked when she saw his blank face.

"Oh yes, sure," he replied. "It's just that you startled me a little." He adjusted himself back into his seat.

She looked at him with confusion in her deep green eyes. "I knocked didn't I?" she asked sheepishly. She was terrified that she'd just intruded on his somewhat private moment.

"Oh yes, sure, don't worry about it," he said with a warm smile on his broad face. Although he wanted to maintain a professional work environment, he also did not want to scare the poor girl. He invited her in and decided to find out how her day had been going. She seemed to be very weary of her every move. She must have been really nervous he thought to himself.

She dropped the letters that she had brought him in a neat pile on the correspondents spot on top of his desk and then withdrew her confused self from his presence. He watched anxiously as she left his office. He was secretly anticipating the moment when she would turn around and give him the privilege of watching her perfectly rounded bum as she made her way out of his office.

Over the next few months, Laura spent most of her time in and out of business meetings and working extremely late into the night. She was spending more than half of her day working alongside Mr. Satin. She had never had to work so hard in her entire life; it seemed like all she ever did was work, work, and more work. Soon the dynamic of the relationship changed from a professional one to a more friendly type of relationship; they were now often out having lunch and dinner together. He would call her on a weekend, just to see how her day was going. She did not want to jump to conclusions, but it seemed like he had taken a liking to her. She had been attracted to him from day one, although she hated to admit it to herself. The more time they spent together, the more her attraction for him grew; she now had a full-blown crush on him. But she was terrified to tell him the truth. She did not want to jeopardize what could be the best job she ever had. The pay was amazing and she intended to keep her job. Besides word around the office was that he was a married man. For her that meant that they could never have a long prosperous relationship. He was already taken.

As Laura sat at her desk mechanically clicking the keys on her laptop, she glanced over at the small clock on the wall. "Darn, nine o'clock," she muttered to herself. Today had been one of those days. She had been at work from eight in the morning, and now it was nine in the evening, and she was nowhere done completing her reports for the day. Thankfully for her, she was not in a serious relationship nor did she have any kids waiting for her at the house. These long hours at the office seemed to be the norm during recent months. She sighed as she continued typing, hoping to be done in about an hour. The knock on the door was sudden and as she hoisted her head, her eyes met his.

"C'mon let's get out of here. You've done enough for today." He had a serious look on his face, one that almost had her worried.

Laura hesitated a little. "I just wanted to finish this off before the shareholders meeting tomorrow," she informed him.

But he was not having it, he wanted her to drop everything and leave. "You need to relax sometime. Too much work and no play makes Laura a dull girl," he said with a chuckle.

A soft smile graced her lips as she tried to quickly wrap up what she was doing. "You need a ride home? The weather's horrible outside," he told her cautiously.

She had been so busy at work that she had not even noticed all the snow outside. Laura finally rose from her seat and walked over to her small window, parting the blinds to take a peek outside. Everywhere was covered in snow. How would she get home? Her car had been down for about a month now. The worried look on her face must have influenced him to offer her a ride home again, for the second time. Any other day she would have said no, but considering the situation she had no choice but to accept his offer.

As they drive off into the night, the flashing lights in the distance soon caught their attention. They could see several cars making U-turns in the distance and driving by. "What's going on?" she asked with a curious look on her face. Mr. Satin drove closer to where the assembly of cars were; there they saw the cause of all the commotion. There had been a major accident, a pile up with about five cars. They could see to the beginning of the deadly collision where there was a huge log truck that had slid off the slippery road.

"What's going on here, officer?" Mr. Satin asked the uniformed policeman who had been walking by.

"We had to block off the road ahead because of the accident. We are trying to get the road clear now," the policeman replied solemnly. He was a tall African American man, with a lean athletic body.

"Oh Gosh, you think anybody died?" Laura asked with a concerned look on her face. She hated vehicular accidents; people almost always lost their lives or the lives of their loved ones. To her a motor vehicular accident was one of the worst ways to die. Upon hearing her question, Mr. Satin peeked outside his window and called out to the same policeman he had been speaking with.

"Is anybody hurt real bad, officer?" he

asked.

The man walked back to the car, removing his police cap on his head, exposing his bald head. He ran his hand over his head before answering. The look on his face seemed to already hint the answer to Mr. Satin's question. "Five dead so far, sir and three others in critical condition. It's the worst we've seen in years," he replied.

"Oh my God! Five dead!" Laura shrieked in disbelief. She hoped that none of her family and friends were involved in this deadly collision. The next thing she did was dial her mom's number to confirm that everyone was fine. In the event that any of her family members or friends had been hurt, Laura wanted to find out now instead of later, when she arrived at their house. Thankfully, her mother Angel put her mind to rest, assuring her that everyone at the house was safe.

As she spoke with her mother, something dawned upon her. The road leading to her home had been completely blocked off because of the accident. They could either sit in the car and wait for the next few hours until the road was cleared or they could turn around and take the back road to her house, which would be a two-hour drive almost. She looked over at Mr. Satin, trying to figure out how she would break the news to him.

"So what do you want to do now?" he asked her. It seemed like he had read her thoughts.

"I'm not sure, do you want to wait or take the back road which is about a two-hour drive," she informed him.

"Neither," he replied in a firm voice. Laura

could not believe her ears. Was he going to drop her off right there on the side of the road and go home? What did he mean when he said neither?

He looked at her pensively before making his next statement. "How about this. How about you come to my apartment for a while, and I will drop you off later when everything has died down," he now had a warm smile on his face. She knew that she could trust him and so she happily accepted his offer. He quickly followed the suit of several of the cars that had been before him, and right there in the middle of the road, he did a sharp U-turn. He sped down the road, ignoring the caution signs that were lined up along the roadside. It took those about fifteen minutes to get to his condo. He lived in one of the high-rise buildings in the center of the city.

"I live on the fifth floor," he said to her as they walked through the lobby. Surprising he walked past the elevator to the red door on the side. "I hope you don't mind; I always take the stairs," he said, pushing the door forward. Several flights of narrow stairs awaited them. Had it been anyone else trying to get her to walk up that flight of stairs, Laura would have said no, but being that he was the one who signed her paychecks, and he had been so kind as to let her stay over at his place, she decided to swallow her pride and march up the stairs behind him. He stopped abruptly, pulling out his key card and swiping the side of a huge brown door.

Laura almost gasped at the sight of his room. It was simply exquisite, more luxurious than any room or house that she had ever seen before. The décor was that of modern architecture mixed with a sophisticated European design. There were huge paintings of a man on the wall; as she examined the paintings, she realized that they were portraits of Mr. Satin in various positions. In one of them he was leaning back into his huge leather chair, while the other was a portrait of him playing golf dressed in a more casual attire. He must have really had a liking to watching huge paintings of him, Laura thought to herself as her eyes caught wind of the thrived and forth portrait of him that hang on the wall along the staircase.

"Can I get you something to drink or something to eat while you wait?" his voice was calm and humble, different from his firm authoritative tone that he would use while at work.

"Oh, some water would be fine thanks," she replied politely.

Within a matter of seconds, he was back from his kitchen offering a glass of water on a small silver tray. Laura felt flattered that he would serve her in that manner. He invited her to have a sit with him on his huge leather sofa, pulling out the small television remote from between the cushions.

"I'm sorry it's a bit messy in here; it's been a while since I've had company over," he said with a slight smile on his face. "Let me go freshen up," he said and disappeared upstairs, returning after about twenty minutes with a white T-shirt and a pair of jeans. He smelt so good, like a breath of fresh air. It was quite a different look from what she was used to seeing him wear. He was usually dressed in expensive professional looking suits, but this casual look also complemented his body perfectly.

Laura looked around curiously. His apartment was far from messy, and it was very well organized, much neater than hers. He must have really been a neat freak if he thought that the apartment was messy as it was. They soon engaged in lively conversation, and for the first time he opened up to her about his life, his wife, and how he started his career. Laura was shocked to hear that his wife had just got up one day and left him for a younger man. Was she insane? He was quite a catch. Why would any woman would leave a man like Chris Satin? she wondered to herself.

As they sat there talking, Laura noticed that he was gradually moving in closer to her. Finally, his body was less than an inch away from hers. Almost suddenly he stopped talking and openly expressed his feelings toward her; she too found the courage to let him know that she'd been attracted to him from day one.

She did not know where the situation with him would end up, but she was willing to explore. As their lips met, a wave of pleasure coursed through her body, and she ached for more of him. His lips caressed hers gently; occasionally, he would suck onto her lower lip, pulling on it softly as his hands roamed all over her body. She moaned and panted as his tongue pleasured her from within her mouth. The more they kissed, the greater their desire for each other became. Soon he was stripping her of her clothes, desperate to consummate with her. The feeling of the cool air on her naked flesh let her know that she was completely naked. Suddenly, he pulled away from her.

"Not like this," he said in a husky desire-filled voice.

He quickly rose to his feet and led her into a huge bedroom. The bedroom was even more lavishly decorated than the other parts of the condo. There he scooped her in his arms and laid her naked body on the huge king-size bed. As Laura lay naked on the bed, she closed her eyes and gave in to his tender touches. Chris was just the type of man that she had been looking for all her life. He was mature, well established, and seemed to know how to make love to a woman. Chris began to gently bite each nipple, moving from breast to breast and then gently kissing each. Laura moaned softly and soon opened her eyes, watching as he fondled her perky melon-shaped breasts. She watched as he supported his weight with his huge muscular arms. He caressed her nipples over and over until she let out an even louder moan. His hand traveled up and down her body, stroking her flesh gently. He spread her legs apart.

"You are dripping wet, baby" he blurted out with a shocked look on his face as his fingers stroked her moist flesh.

He continued to stroke her flesh, bringing about unimaginable sensations upon Laura. He used his thumb and forefinger to caress her flesh. After a while he pulled away and stood up, ridding himself of the T-shirt and jeans that he had been wearing. His dick was released and Laura almost gasped at its length and size. It looked amazing! It was golden brown with large dark veins running across it. She licked her lips, desperate to take it into her hungry mouth. It seemed longer and bigger than any other dick she had ever seen in her whole life. He returned to his former position and he explored almost every inch of her naked body with his tongue. She moaned and moaned as sensations gripped her body, causing her to surrender to his every touch. How could he have had such an effect on her?

Now that she had felt him all over her body, Laura knew she needed to feel him inside her pussy. He pulled away once more and rose to his feet to take a sip from her glass of water she had placed on his right stand. As he enjoyed the drink of water, his eyes carefully examined every inch of her naked body. He gave her a wicked little grin as he took another sip of water. Laura signaled him with her index finger to come to her, while she pleasured herself with her other hand, rubbing onto her swollen clit and then moaning with pleasure. As he watched her pleasure herself, his dick throbbed in anticipation of penetrating her wet pussy. He used his hand and stroked his cock a few times as he licked his lips.

"You want this little, tight pussy?" Laura teased as she used her finger to spread her pink pussy lips. She let out a series of loud pleasurable moans as she continued to thrust her finger in and out of her wetness.

Chris looked at her with longing in his eyes;

he was impressed at her boldness. She seemed like she would not be able to survive one more minute without his dick inside her pussy. Talking about her pussy, he looked at it carefully as he came closer to her. It was pretty pink, and the clitoris was tiny, almost hidden away. It was a tiny little pussy. He slowly came between her legs and kissed her softly on her clitoris.

"You're gorgeous, you know that?" he said breathlessly as his desires got the best of him. He had promised himself that he would never have another office romance, but here he was with this very attractive young woman who was making it impossible to stay away from her.

"Really?" Laura whispered with her wicked smile. She knew that she was an attractive young woman, but hearing someone like Chris Satin compliment her on her beauty heightened her arousal. She wanted nothing more than to please him. He could have had any one of the other girls in the office, hell anyone other woman as a matter of fact, but yet here he was with her. Finally, he walked toward her and leaned in over her. His lips came crashing down on hers, and she almost melted at the feel of his hot body on hers. His lips soon left hers and he caressed her along the nape of her neck. Laura moaned; it felt like it was all too much for her to bear. He was also panting heavily as his tongue explored the nape of her neck. After a while his tongue traveled downward from the nape of her neck to her hardened nipples, taking them in one by one with his mouth. She moaned out for more. He obviously knew what he was doing; he knew how to stroke her body in all the right places that seemed to have her almost to the point of exploding. Finally, he trailed downward to her temple of delight with his hot wet tongue. Chris began to passionately kiss her pussy, firstly, licking it back and forth, then spreading it with his fingers, and trying to suck the pussy hole itself.

"OH MY GOD!" Laura screamed with ecstasy. "Oh baby, just like that, don't stop," she bucked her pussy up against his mouth as he continued to pleasure her with his tongue.

Laura found herself getting louder and louder, demanding exactly how she wished to be pleasured.

"Oh yeah, lick that pussy," she said as her legs began to shake and she lost herself in the feeling of Chris' tongue on and inside her pussy.

Chris was thoroughly enjoying sucking Laura's pussy, but he knew she was enjoying it even more. He intended to make her cum harder than she had ever cum before in her life. He began pulling on the clit with his tongue, back and forth, as if trying to suck it off.

"Oh, Chris," he heard her moan as she cupped his head between her hands. "Don't stop, baby, don't stop," she begged as she closed her eyes clenched her teeth together. He sucked on her clitoris even harder, elated at the way her body was reacting to his tongue.

"Oh yeah," she moaned as her fingers

gripped the sheets. In all her life she had never felt anything this amazing. She had had guys perform oral sex on her, but none of them seemed to have been able to make her body quiver the way Chris was making it. He seemed to be an expert in that field; his years of experience were showing with every stroke that he gave her.

Chris stopped and pulled his head back a little and watched her pussy. The clitoris was now swollen, double the size it was when he started; her pussy was so wet, he could see the wetness on the sheets under her butt. He came over her and looked directly into her eyes and said with a wicked smile, “Why are you so wet? I have not even begun fucking you yet.” He could not believe how wet her pussy was; she had been such as quiet reserved young woman. Never in his wildest dreams had he imagined a day like this one, where she would be on his bed all wet and bothered. As Laura opened her eyes, she locked gazes with him.

His eyes were now darker than ever and filled with desire. She could tell that he caressing her pussy with his tongue was just the preamble to something even better that was yet to come. Her body ached for everything that he had to offer, and she desperately wanted, needed, to feel his shaft penetrating her tight pussy. His dick had looked so huge and hard, and she felt her urge to fuck him intensify as images of his massive nature seemed to plague her mind. Laura decided that the best thing she could do was surrender her body to him and let him pleasure her just how he wanted to without interrupting him. “Baby, this pussy is yours to do whatever, enjoy,” she moaned with a wicked little smile forming in the corner of her mouth. She did mean every word that she had said. She wanted nothing more in the world than to her body abused and rammed by his cock.

While she would have loved to have him continue sucking her pussy until she came, she knew that she wanted to fuck him just as bad. She wanted to feel his long hard dick inside her pussy, and so she began to gently caress his dick with her hands, slowly first and then faster. She could hear him panting louder and louder as his dick began to increase in its erection. She could literally feel his massive cock throbbing against the palm of her hands. The huge bulging veins seemed to be pulsating as she stroked him with her hand. At that moment she forgot about everything else; she just wanted to be with him.

“I want to taste your dick,” she said to him.

Chris immediately stood at the edge of the bed with his dick in his hand and replied, “Come get it, baby.”

Laura slowly moved toward him and sat at the edge of the bed, and she began to kiss his dick softly, making pleasurable sounds as she went along. Then she licked it, first licking up and down, from the head down to his balls.

“Oh baby, you’re the best,” Chris moaned as he tilted his head back and took a deep breath.

She then proceeded to put the entire dick

into her mouth, going down and down on it, to the point where she gagged and almost spit on it.

"Take your time, baby, you try to swallow the entire thing," he said with a smile on his face.

He knew he did not have the world's biggest dick, but she knew his dick was definitely one of the world's longest dicks. Laura, upon hearing this, decided it was time to cut that smile from his face and make him moan like a baby. She began to suck his dick long and hard as if sucking a delicious lollipop. He groaned with pleasure at her new technique. He cupped her head in both his hands as if to help her with her head movements. She then stopped sucking the entire dick and began to lick the head of the dick around the edges, then flicked her tongue back and forth around the head of the dick. She knew that kind of stuff drove him crazy.

"Oh God, Laura, damn!" he said with sounds of pleasure in his voice.

She then went back to sucking his dick long and hard, as if trying to get the cum out of it. She could see his knees shaking, and she knew that he was enjoying it.

"Laura, stop, you are going to make me cum," he said almost as if trying to stop an accident from happening. He picked her off the bed and with her legs wrapped around him; he kissed her passionately, then he laid her on the bed. He spread her legs open and then climbed on top of her immediately, as if with no control. Then he slammed his dick inside her wet pussy.

"Oh baby," she shrieked. He realized that her pussy was incredibly tight, almost like she was a virgin. He wanted to ask but he decided against it. From his experience some women would get offended if they were asked whether they were virgins or not.

"I am sorry, baby," he said kissing her softly on her forehead. He then gently removed his dick and slid it in slowly this time, locking gazes with her as he penetrated her pussy.

"Oh that feels so good," he said. Chris finally began to slowly fuck her. He closed his eyes as if trying to concentrate on what he was doing. Several loud groans escaped his lips as she moaned with every stroke and thrust that he gave her. He was happy to see and hear that the pleasure was mutual; she too was enjoying the moment. He could see her head was cocked back against the pillow, with her eyes shut tightly; he heard her moan making. The sounds of her "oohs" and "awwwsss" almost drove him insane. She looked so different lying naked on his bed. It was almost like night and day. She had always seemed so poised and calm with hair pulled back neatly into a pony tail, but now her hair was all messy as she moaned loudly to the feel of his dick.

As he penetrated her moist heat, the desire that he had for her intensified and so did his groans and his thrusting. Chris felt the need to explode his load of cum inside of her moistness. He gripped firmly onto her hips and gave her several hard thrusts that had the bed jerking back and forth against the wall of his room. He wondered if anyone could hear them in the euphoric moment. She must have sensed that he was ready to cum because she began grinding her hips as he pounded her pussy. He felt like he was losing all control as his dick got harder and hotter inside her pussy.

Laura moaned out, unable to control her movements anymore. The delirium of the moment gripped her, and she could feel his strokes become longer and harder, and then quicker and harder.

"Oh Laura, my God!" he groaned giving her an intense look.

"Yes, baby, give it to me," she responded desperately, as if pleading for something good. He stealthy flipped her over, with her ass propped out toward him. He wanted to change his technique a little and try something new. A loud shriek escaped her lips as her body tensed up against his grip.

Laura had done anal sex a few times in the past, but it had always been so painful and she had also ended up saying she would never try it again. Now that she was with Chris; she had wanted to stop but found herself unable to resist him. She wanted everything that this man had to offer. She gripped the sheets between her teeth and closed her eyes tightly, hoping that the pain would soon go away.

Chris could not believe how tight she was in the back. It almost seemed like the muscles in her anus were restricting the entry of his dick. He gripped firmly onto her beautifully rounded bum and with a mighty thrust penetrated her anus, thrusting his dick all the way inside. She wailed out in pain. He was quite shocked to hear the words coming out of her once so innocent mouth. She was swearing at him. He ignored her rants and continued to fuck her asshole. He soon increased the momentum of his thrusts, and soon, he felt the urge to smack her ass. Without hesitation he gave her a hard smack on the ass. This time she screamed out calling for God to help her. All her crying and moaning was increasing his arousal and in the moment he wanted to see and hear her beg him to stop. But unfortunately she did no such thing. In fact she was so wasteful that she found a way to bare the pain of his anal torture. She had managed to slip her hand between her thighs and was now gently rubbing against her clitoris and simulating herself.

Her painful moans were now replaced by pleasurable ones as she continued to pleasure herself. As she rubbed against her clitoris, she could feel her juices trickling down her pussy. The sensations and feelings that were running through her body felt amazing. She moaned out loud, begging Chris to continue. Her body quivered as he penetrated her anus over and over with his long shaft. It was almost too much for her to handle. She found herself closing her eyes as she gripped the sheets for support. Suddenly, he increased the momentum of his thrusts, and he was now plunging his kick inside her asshole, causing her to moan out even louder than before.

“Oh, Oh, I’m cum– I’m cuming…” he groaned as he gave her one last hard jolt and exploded inside her.

She in turn, screamed “Oh yes!” with

pleasure, and their bodies jolted and climaxed together. She could feel the hot cum running from his dick inside her.

"Oh, my God that was amazing!" he said as he kissed her on her forehead.

She kissed him back and replied "I know it was. Thank you." They both were exhausted and laid next to each other naked, while sleep engulfed them.

Laura woke up to the sound of a phone ringing. As she opened her eyes, she realized that she was not in her room. Where the heck was she? Her eyes perused her new environment, trying to recognize the place.

"Hey. Good morning beautiful," a voice called out. She looked straight ahead and her eyes fell upon the strikingly handsome Chris Satin. He was making his way out of the shower with a white towel wrapped around his waist.

"I didn't want to wake you; you looked so peaceful in bed," he said with a warm smile on his face. Laura soon realized what had happened; she had slept with her boss. A wave of panic rushed through her body. What if he decided to fire her? What if he were just using her? So many questions lingered on her mind. She quickly sat upright and ran her hands through her silky hair. What would she do now that she had slept with her boss?

He must have been able to sense the fear on her face. "Don't worry, you still have your job," he laughed. Laura had to admit this was one of the first things that crossed her mind when she woke and saw that they had slept together.

"Are you sure?" she teased. He gave out a loud laugh and then walked up to her, handing her the extra cup of coffee that he had been holding in one hand. "I was not sure how you liked your coffee," he said as he handed her the brown cup.

Surprisingly, he had got it just right. In fact, his coffee tasted even better than hers. As she sipped on the coffee, he slipped closer to her and assured her that everything was okay. She had been shaking like a leaf, terrified of what would happen to her now that she had crossed the line with her boss. He gave her a soft kiss on the neck.

"It's okay, relax," he whispered to her, as he placed his coffee on the night stand and proceeded to pleasure her with his tongue on her neck. Her body quivered at the feeling of his tongue on her flesh. She gave him her cup of coffee, and soon they locked lips together in a hot wet passionate kiss. That morning yet again, they made love right there in his room. And it was amazing. It seemed surreal to Laura. Never in her wildest dreams did she ever think that she would be intimately involved with Mr. Satin. He had seemed to be such an uptight guy when they first met, but as time had gone by, he had turned out to be the perfect gentleman. That day Laura did not even go to work, and the best part about it was she did not have to call in since she was with her boss. Their day started out great with their lovemaking session at his condo. Then they went shopping. He gave her his credit card to splurge with and to get her a new wardrobe. Which she happily did.

Later on during the day, they had lunch at an exquisite little Italian restaurant. They culminated their day with a long stroll in the park while feeding the ducks. For the first time in her life, Laura had met a guy who enjoyed doing most of the things that she herself enjoyed doing like long walks in the park, eating fancy Italian dishes, and just in general being a very nice supportive individual. After their stroll in the park, they went back to his apartment, and there they watched a movie together before having some fun in the kitchen cooking.

If there was one thing that Laura was incapable of doing that would be cooking. She watched as he baked his pork chops and cooked his rice and beans. "I can't wait to taste it all," she said, prancing back and forth in the kitchen anxious to taste the meals he had prepared. He seemed to be a very good chef. Laura was pleasantly surprised; she never thought that she would see him behind a cooker cooking and baking stuff for them to enjoy. The dinner preparations took about two hours before they were ready, and when everything was all done, he left briefly and went into the small wine cellar he had hidden in the back of his kitchen and soon returned with a huge bottle of wine in his hand.

"Here's the wine to complement it all," he said jokingly. She had never seen him in such a relaxed fun-filled mood; it was like he was not the Chris Satin that she knew from work. It almost seemed like she was dealing with his secret twin brother.

That night the two of them just relaxed and

played several board games together, including Monopoly, chess, and snakes and ladders. They were getting to know each other on a more intellectual level. They spoke about everything from past relationships to work, to what their future goals and objectives were. Laura mentioned the fact that she hoped to one day own a company much like himself. Surprisingly, his goal was to one day find a woman that would love and appreciate him no matter how hard he worked. Laura's heart went out to him. How could any woman not love such an ambitious hardworking man and how could any mature woman want to break up with him and go be with another guy?

Over the next few weeks, Laura and Chris became incredibly close. They would often sneak off from work and go out to a fancy little restaurant to have lunch and go over their day. He also reduced the workload that he had been giving to her. He was now more patient and understanding with her. She worked her best nonetheless, giving him more than one hundred percent of herself. He saw her hard work and dedication and really appreciated everything that she did for him. He would shower her with expensive gifts and jewelry, and everyone in the office soon found out about their relationship and they did not seem to mind.

Although she was still pretty young, Laura found herself contemplating and hoping that she would be able to start a family with Chris in the near future. He had told her about his ex-wife, and how she did not want to have any kids. At first Laura found it hard to believe but as time when by and she got to know him, she realized that he was just an all-round good guy, and it was definitely possible that his wife would try to take advantage of him, since she had been so manipulative.

They were now practically living together, and she was always over at his huge apartment. They were coming out of the grocery store engaged in lively chatter when she saw the look on his face change. He was on a call that had just come in on his cell phone. Clearly, whatever or whoever he was speaking to on the phone was getting him pretty worked up. He motioned her to move forward while he found a quiet little spot on the side of the store. She watched him curiously. Thankful she could read lips; she stood from the distance and tried to make out what words he was saying.

"What? You are pregnant!" she saw his mouth say. Her heart sank. She did not know what was going on. Was he cheating on her? And if so, who was he cheating on her with was an even better question. It seemed like her world was coming crashing down upon her, and she did not know what to do or how to approach the situation. She waited when he was done on the phone before she asked him any questions with regard to his mysterious phone call. Laura stood there, in shock, when he divulged the details of his conversation to her. It was his ex-wife Amy; she had called to inform him that she was with child.

A few weeks later Laura had the shock of her life while at work. A tall brunette woman walked into her office. Her condition was very visible.

"Are you Laura?" she asked with curiosity in her dark brown eyes.

Laura hesitated a little before answering this stranger. She wanted to know why this mysterious woman was trying to find her out. Finally, she answered with a simple "Yes."

The woman's eyes intensified as she kept a straight face while looking at Laura. "I need you to stop seeing my husband. Whatever relationship you have with him, end it now," she said firmly.

Laura's eyes widened with disbelief, and it took her a while to figure out who the woman was. But she had to confirm who she was. "Mrs. Satin, right?" Laura asked with curious eyes. The woman gave Laura a long pensive look before confirming her identity.

"Yes, that's right. I want you to end whatever you have going on with my husband Chris Satin. Okay?" she said with a serious look on her face.

Laura's heart raced at this sudden confrontation. She'd been having a good day at work up until that moment. If she had been a good girl, she would have been able to deny the whole thing. But she could not. Over the months she had developed very strong feelings for Mr. Satin, and she could not just play it off and walk away from it all. Yes, his wife seemed intimidating, but she was not about to back down to the woman who had walked out on him and broke his heart.

She needed to stand up to this woman. Laura managed to muster up the courage to admit to her relationship with Mr. Satin. She could not allow the woman's bold fearless attitude to scare her. She even went further by saying that she loved him, and they were going to be with each other, no matter what.

"Nothing or no one will come in between Chris and me, ma'am. I am not going to just forget about him because you ask me to walk away," Laura confirmed as she diverted her attention to the work she had been doing on her computer before the intrusion on her privacy.

The woman moved in closer to her and spoke with much emphasis at Laura. "I'm warning you woman. I won't come back here to warn you again. Stay away from my husband. We are about to have a baby and I do not need a little skank like you hanging around my man," the woman threatened Laura. She gently massaged her swollen stomach with small circular motions with one hand while maintaining a steady gaze at Laura.

Just as things started getting heated up, "What's going on over here?" a powerful masculine voice called out from the doorway.

Both women turned their attention to the man standing in the door. Mr. Satin took a few strides and positioned himself in the middle of the two angry women. He had a curious look on his face as he switched his gaze from one woman to the next.

Laura answered first. "Your wife over here

has a problem with me," she said pointing her index finger at the older more mature-looking woman. "She wants me to stay away from you. She came here to warn me I guess," Laura continued looking at Mr. Satin directly in the eye as she spoke.

"What are you doing here, Amy? I told you we would talk later at the house," Mr. Satin gave her an annoyed look. His voice had a hint of irritation in it.

"She needed to know the truth, Chris. You are about to be a dad, and I do not want you sleeping around with your secretary," his wife said glancing over at Laura and giving her a wicked little smile.

"Not now, Amy. This is not the time or the place," he shot back at her with an even angrier tone of voice than before. He would have told Laura about her on his own time. But being the manipulative woman that she was, Amy was determined to destroy whatever relationship that her husband was having with this younger woman. At the moment she actually envied Laura for her youthful nature.

Laura watched as the two argued back and forth with each other - insulting each other even, each blaming the other for their failed relationship.

"You did this to us," Mr. Satin argued. "You walked out on me, remember? To be with a younger man. Where is he at now?"

"You worked like a slave, Chris. What did you expect me to do? I had to move on. I'm sorry. I could not stay," she shot back at him.

Laura continued watching the husband and wife argue. It was clear that there were a lot of unresolved issues between the couple. The more she looked on, the sicker she became. She needed to escape from it all. She quickly rose to her feet and rushed past the two of them, leaving them alone in the office to continue with their bickering. They were so consumed in their disagreement that Mr. Satin had not even realized that Laura had left the room. That afternoon when she got back to work, her world was shattered during a conservation with Mr. Satin.

He had come to her office sheepishly with a sad look on his face. His words seemed cold and emotionless.

"I cannot continue our relationship. I can't continue seeing you anymore, Laura," he said with his head bent down in shame. He could not even lift his head to look her in the eye.

"I'm sorry, but Amy and I are getting back together. We are going to try to work on our marriage, for our baby's sake," he continued.

"What?!" Laura exclaimed as her emotions got the best of her. She felt a mixture of negative energy toward him. She felt sad, upset, and disappointed all at the same time.

"How could you do this to me?" she wailed while bursting into tears right there before him.

His facial expression changed from a cold emotionless one to a look of compassion and remorse. The worst part of it all was the fact that she had now fallen deeply in love with him. Even worse was the fact that he was doing exactly what his wife had done to him to her. Did he not remember how hurt he had been when she had walked out on him? How can he turn around and do to her exactly what had been done to him?

"How can you hurt me like that?" she wailed. Her voice was filled with pain. A stream of tears were making their way down the sides of her cheeks as she tried to calm herself down.

He moved in closer to her, and with an earnest look on his face, he tried to explain to her the reason for his actions. "I've always wanted to have a baby and I told you that. This is my opportunity to get that life I have always dreamed about," he said.

Laura could hardly believe her ears. She had honestly believed that a day like this would never come. Certainly never in her wildest dreams did she think that he would be the one to break up with her. Another scary thought crossed her mind: how would she be able to come to work every day knowing that she had been dumped by her boss? How would the ambiance of the office be? Would he fire her out of the awkwardness of it all?

"I cannot believe you are doing this to me," Laura squeaked as she picked up her small black bag and left the office hastily.

Mr. Satin sat there in the small chair next to her desk just pondering on the entire situation. Her words seemed to bother him the most; the fact that she compared what he did to her to what his wife had done to him. How could she even compare the two situations? After much consideration, he had to admit to himself that it was kind of shameful the way he had ended his relationship with Laura. She had been the girl who had not done anything mean or hurtful to him, and she had been supportive the entire time. He reminisced about the good times that they had together. He did have very strong feelings toward her. She was always laughing and cheering him on. He had never had this much fun with any other woman, especially not with his wife Amy.

Amy had always kept a serious face, her jokes were very few, and she was always more consumed with herself and what she was doing instead of being supportive toward him. Although she accused him of being a workaholic and ended their relationship saying that it was because he worked too much, she herself was always busy doing something. Between her constant shopping sprees, trips to the spa, and visits to the hair salon, she seemed very busy.

Mr. Satin finally rose out of his seat and exited the door. His heart was heavy from having hurt Laura, the woman that he loved even more than his wife Amy, although he cared greatly for his wife and his unborn child. He loved Laura and up until that incident he wanted to start a life and a family with her.

That evening he went home devastated. As he entered the door, his eyes caught wind of his wife Amy, who was busy at her computer. The little smirk that she had on her faced almost puzzled him, but he soon realized that there was something weird going on and she was up to no good. He quietly crept up behind her, being careful as to not alert her of his presence. He peeked at the computer screen to see what she was doing. Maybe she was secretly watching porn? But no. She had a chat box open. She had been chatting with a guy. Not just any guy, the profile picture on the side of the chat box was that of a young man. Younger than him, younger than her too. He could not understand why she felt the need to be chatting with someone younger than her. His eyes slowly surveyed the screen as he began to read the contents of the conversation between his wife, Amy 40, and the stranger Hot Rod 25.

Hot Rod 25: Hey baby how's your day going? You busy?

Amy 40: I'm doing well my love. How's your day, do you miss me?

Hot Rod 25: Oh, I'm just home chilling. Hell yeah I miss you and that sweet pussy of yours.

Amy 40: You do? I miss you too my love. My hot rod. Lol

Hot Rod 25: What are you doing right now love? I'm really horny right now, can we meet or something.

Amy 40: Yea of course my love. I'm so bored right now. It might help out a great deal if I get a good fuck. Lol. You know this pregnancy is having me horny all the time. Lol.

Hot Rod 25: Yea, it does huh. Lol. I can take care of you baby. Do your body right better than your old man.

Amy 40: The usual place my love, can you be there in ten minutes.

Hot Rod: Yeah sure, you're talking about the motel on Jarrett Street next to the old gas statio, right?.

Amy 40: Yeah, but hurry my husband will

be home soon.

Suddenly, the phone rang and interrupted her conversation. Mr. Satin pulled back but not quickly enough. As she turned around to get the phone, she gasped at the sight of her husband standing behind her. Had he read her conversation?

"Why did you creep up on me?" she asked in an irate tone of voice. His eyes were filled with anger as he answered her question.

"You're online setting up dates with other men? I thought we agreed to stop seeing other people and work things out between us?" he asked with curious eyes.

He was more furious at himself for having trusted her. She had come back into his life with the news of a baby on the way, and he had happily taken her back. And poor Laura, She had been an innocent victim in his complicated love affair. She had been heartbroken when he had ended things with her. It was now becoming more and more apparent to him. He and Amy could never work things out. She was nothing but a lying, conniving, manipulative, self-absorbed woman. At that moment had she not been with child, he would have thrown her out of his condo. There were hundreds of other women that would have loved to be in her place.

His wife tried to deny the entire thing. Saying that she was just joking around with one of her long-time friends. But Mr. Satin was smarter than that; he had read the conversation with his own two eyes. Nothing that she said or did would convince him that she was just joking.

"And to think I broke up with Laura, just to be with you," he told her with a disgusted look on his face. "Laura never did nothing this cruel or mean to me; she was a good girl, faithful and loyal to me, something you have no idea how to be," he continued.

She tried to touch him, but he shrugged away. "Don't touch me, Amy!" he shrieked.

"I'm sorry, baby. It only happened one time. I was just bored, I would never cheat on you again," she said trying desperately to pacify him. But it was all too late. He had made up his mind. In that moment Mr. Satin regretted ever breaking up with Laura just to be with Amy, the woman who had walked out on him.

Finally, he said in a cold emotionless voice, "I can't do this with you anymore, Amy. Not again."

"No, don't. Please stay with me," she begged him.

"Amy, you are never going to change. I cannot continue to let you break my heart like this," he said in a firm voice. With that he strode across the room, making his way to the front door.

Amy burst into tears at the realization that he was now breaking up with her. "What about our baby?" she called out to him, with anger in her voice.

He could hardly believe his ears. He was certain now that she was using her pregnancy to manipulate him. What did she want him to do after what he just saw?

"The baby will be just fine. We don't have to be in a relationship to raise the baby," he assured her. There were many people that he knew who raised their children while divorced. It just depended on having a plan as to how to raise the baby. She cried out to him, begging him to remain with her. She apologized profusely for everything she had done to him, but her apologies fell on deaf ears. He continued walking out the door without even turning behind to look at her. She screamed and wailed at him, but he did not care, he was on a mission to get Laura back.

When he got to Laura's quaint little apartment, Mr. Satin contemplated what he would say to her. How would she ever take him back considering how he had just hurt her. He knocked on the door lightly, terrified of what she would say when she say that he was at her door.

"What are you doing here?" her voice called out from behind the door that was half cracked open. She was peaking between the small spaces.

"I'm sorry, Laura, I should have never..."

Before he even had the opportunity to continue she interrupted him with her hurt filled voice. "I don't care; I don't want to hear anything," she shot at him.

"Go back to your WIFE!" she cried out. Her voice made him quiver. He had never intended to hurt her the way he did. He had to explain everything to her, to try to get her to understand his side of the situation.

"Can I come in? I need to talk to you," he begged. For the first time in his life, he was actually begging someone for something. She did not budge for a minute and kept eying him from behind the door.

"Please, I'm begging you. I love you and I need to talk to you," his voice had a sense of yearning in it that she had never heard before.

Although was extremely hurt by his actions and the past few days had been like living in hell for her, she missed him dearly and she secretly hoped and prayed for him to come back to her. She also had some very interesting news to share with him about the woman that he called his wife. News that she had received from a very valuable source that would discredit everything that she had ever told him.

Finally, she let him in, slowly and carefully watching every step that he took. Mr. Satin breathed a sigh of relief when he entered the apartment. His eyes perused the place; she had made a few changes in her apartment, cleaned up a little.

"I see you made some changes around here," he said to her, in an attempt to break the ice between them.

She simply nodded her head signaling her response. She did not say anything much; she just waited curiously to hear what he had to say. She had determined that she would listen to him, but that did not mean that she would forgive him or take him back. The fact that he could have easily just ended the relationship and let his wife move back in with him was scary to her. She had thought that their relationship meant a lot more to him.

He proceeded to move in closer to her, cupping her face in his hand.

"I'm sorry for putting you through all this," he started. His eyes had a genuine look in them. She could tell that he cared for her by just looking into his deep eyes. He seemed to transfer a feeling of remorse to her without even saying much. His apology seemed sincere and it took everything that she had to fight back the urge to kiss him and let him know that she had forgiven him. No, she told herself. You have to be strong; you cannot be so weak.

He continued to talk to her, "I am so filled with remorse and hurt for what I did; I know that you are hurt, because I know that feeling, I have been there before. The feeling where you love someone who turns you down, just to be with someone you know is not good for them," he continued. He locked gazes with her and continued to intoxicate her with his words.

Laura finally spoke to him. "What hurt the most was the fact that you made it seem so easy, you just walked away from me, without even trying to work things out," her voice was cracked as a line of tears made their way down the side of her face.

"Laura, I don't want anybody else but you, whether they are with child or not, I just want you," he assured her as his lips came crashing down upon hers. She wanted desperately to pull away, to curse at him for what he had done, but she could not. This was a man whom she had loved dearly, a man whom she could never find herself walking out on. Their tongues danced together in the ecstasy of the moment. As the passion within consumed the both of them, their hands roamed freely all over each other's bodies. His hand stroked her body, and soon they were both stripping each other of their clothes.

Laura gave a little moan as his tongue made contact with her bare skin along the nape of her neck. He kissed and teased almost every inch of her gorgeous long neck. He continued his trail down along her body and soon found her perfectly rounded breasts. He focused his attention on their hardened nipples, taking them into his mouth and fondling them with his tongue. Laura moaned some more as tiny spasms rushed through her body, causing her juices to saturate the thin lace thong that she had been wearing.

Mr. Satin continued to caress her body, and soon his fingers traveled upward between her tights until it reached her moist core. He gently stroked her wet pussy with two of his fingers while he continued to suck onto her breasts, one nipple at a time. The sensations that he was bringing about seemed almost unbearable. Laura's body ached for the feel of his shaft inside her. She moaned out loud, begging him to penetrate her core with his massive cock. He did not hesitate and immediately filled her up with his dick.

He braced her up against the wall and served her with several hard upward thrusts that had her in pure ecstasy. Over and over he penetrated her pussy, while groaning out and whispering sweet confessions to her.

"I love you, Laura," he whispered as he gave her a hard upward thrust. His lips soon captured hers and her moans were muffled by his hot wet tongue. He devoured her with his mouth and her body quivered for more. His dick penetrated her pussy over and over again. The entire time she moaned and begged him to fuck her harder. He gave her a series of short hard thrusts mixed with slow longer ones. Soon he increased his momentum and lost himself in the delirium of the moment. With a mighty hard thrust, he penetrated deep inside her, causing her to let out a loud stretched moan as he too exploded inside her pussy. She propped up against the wall tired and spent from it all.

"Forgiven," she teased him. He smiled and leaned in, planting a soft kiss upon her forehead. He had loved her more than anything else in the world. His lips met hers as he swept her in a hot wet passionate kiss. She led him to the bedroom upstairs and lay next to him, cuddling in his sweet embrace. They soon dozed off into the night.

Chris almost gasped at the feel of her hands on his hard cock. Her mouth soon followed her hands as she took hold of his shaft with her hungry lips. "Laura!" his groan was husky as he opened his sleepy eyes. He had been sleeping and awakened by the feel of her lips on his dick.

Laura had always been an innovative person, and she enjoyed seeing him quiver at her caress. She had been planning this secret attack on his dick for a few weeks now. And she was happy that he seemed to be enjoying it so far.

She took him in and out of her hot mouth. Lavishing his huge cock with her tongue, stroking it all over. She gave his cock a combination of long gentle strokes followed by harder shorter sucks. Another groan escaped his lips as she cupped his balls with her hand, gently massaging them. His penis throbbed in anticipation of penetrating her sweet pussy.

"I want it now, Laura," he begged as he felt the throbbing between his legs intensify with every passing minute. Never in his life had he been awakened by a woman who had her tongue on his shaft.

She did not hesitate, and in an instant she mounted his hard cock and plummeted her wet pussy over his shaft. She rocked her body gently against his as she rode his dick over and over again. Her moans were loud, and she was occasionally whispering obscenities to him, begging him to fuck her harder. Chris closed his eyes and gripped onto her perfectly rounded ass, serving her with a series of hard upward thrusts that had her moaning. He let out another loud groan as he closed his eyes, taking in some air.

Over the months Laura had learnt a lot about him, so much so that she knew his body; she knew what made him tingle, what made him shiver, and what made him cum. She continued riding his penis just the way he liked, slowly thrusting and pushing down on his cock and then increasing her momentum. Her beautiful black hair draped her gorgeous long neck, and her melon-shaped breasts bounced up and down as she rode his cock.

She used her thumb and her index finger to gently pinch and rub against his nipples. As she caressed him by playing with his nipples, he panted heavily, shoving his cook upward inside her moist heat.

She was now also moaning as she rocked her pussy viciously against him. Her insides were hot and moist, and Chris could feel her juices trickling down on his erection. He could also feel the tiny spasms that seemed to be escaping her pussy and running through his penis. She increased her momentum once more, bucking her pussy viciously against his raw meat. She could feel his dick getting harder and harder inside her as he increased the momentum of his upward thrusts inside her pussy.

"Oh, yes!" she moaned as she closed her eyes and tilted her head back.

She gave in to the delirium of the moment, surrendering her body to him. Chris could hardly control himself; he began to heave his body from the bed, thrusting his penis upward inside her. She shrieked out in pain at first, but then her cries changed. They were now moans of pleasure. He gripped firmly onto her hips and gave her a series of several hard upward thrusts. Laura went wild and she started moaning obscenities at him. She had always been so prim and proper in public but a total whore in the bedroom. The changes in her attitude had taken him by storm; he had realized that after a few weeks of being with her around the office that she would quiet and settled, then while in his bed she would be loud and wild. He had nothing against her change in attitude though; in fact he actually liked watching her transform. It was like she was being consumed with her desires and changing from this quiet young woman into a loud deadly dragon.

"Oh Chris, harder! Tear that fucking pussy up!" she begged him.

Her voice was filled with desire and her eyes seemed to be even hungrier than her pussy. Chris could not resist the sudden urge to kiss her, the urge to block her filthy little mouth. His lips come crashing down on her as his tongue swept through her desire-filled mouth. Her body quivered at the feeling of his tongue. Chris could also feel the tiny contractions that had increased in waves on his penis; her pussy is hungry for him. He had to satisfy it.

With a swift movement he rolled her over and they had switched positions. He was now on top of her. His penis was thrilled and as he penetrated her pussy, the room was filled with the sounds of her moaning ceaselessly. Her fingers dug into the flesh of his back as he served her with a series of hard long strokes. Her pussy was dripping wet, and he felt tiny spasms making their way from her temple of delight and onto his massive cock. He had to close his eyes to really just enjoy and savor the moment that resulted from fucking her pussy.

"Oh God, I'm gonna cum!" she moaned as she closed her eyes and clenched her teeth. He increased his momentum and the big king-sized bed was jerking up and down as he gave her a series of hard wild thrusts. Over and over he thrust his penis inside her wet cunt, causing her to moan louder and louder.

Finally, he let out a loud thunderous groan, and with a mighty thrust, he exploded his load of cum inside her. Soon after she also let out a long stretched moan and summited her climax. Exhausted, he rolled over to her side and lied upward gazing at the ceiling.

"Wow, that was amazing!" she said as she placed her head on his bare chest. Laura finally got up and headed for the shower.

When she got out of the shower, Laura decided to tell Mr. Satin the news that she had heard from her friend down at the lab. She asked him to sit down to deliver the devastating news. Her friend had seen his wife come into the doctor's office with another man, to do her regular checkup. The guy had identified himself as the baby's father. He was a younger guy, just like the one Mr. Satin had described to her. Mr. Satin gasped, covering his mouth with the palm of his hand. Although it sounded unbelievable, it was very real. It was actually starting to make sense. Thinking back he was now realizing that it would be somewhat impossible Amy to have gotten pregnant by him, unless she was carrying the baby for a ten-month term. Before she had left him, they barely had sex that month.

He could not believe it; she had tried to con him with a baby that was not even his.

"I can't believe this," he said shaking his head. "How could she even do this to me," his voice was filled with hurt and sadness.

It was then that Laura decided to share the other part of news with him. Over the past three weeks, she had been feeling very ill. She had finally gone to see a doctor who had run some test on her. Surprisingly, the test confirmed that she was indeed two months pregnant.

"What?" Mr. Satin's eyes lit up. He could hardly sit still. "How? When? Oh my God!" he exclaimed. His voice was filled with excitement in it. She had been keeping it a secret from him, not wanting to destroy whatever plans that he had with his wife. She had even decided that she would raise her illegitimate child in another state, so as to prevent any awkwardness.

He leaned in and embraced her softly as a small stream of tears made their way down the side of his face. He was now truly the happiest man alive. He had everything he wanted. Well almost.

Laura's eyes popped open at the site of him dropping down to his knees. "What are you doing?" she asked with curiosity in her eyes.

"I've wanted to do this for a while," he said with a smile on his face. "I know my divorce is not final or anything, but at least this will let you know that I am one hundred percent committed to you, and nothing or no one will come in between us again." With that said, he pulled out a beautiful diamond ring from the small black box he had holding in his hand.

She gasped at the sight of the most beautiful and exquisite ring that she had ever seen in her life.

"Will you marry me and raise a family with me, Laura?" he asked with a look of longing in his eyes.

She gave him a warm smile, excited that he would even think about making her his new wife. “Yes, of course! I cannot think of anything else I’d rather be doing for the rest of my life,” she said to him with a sincere look.

Mr. Satin felt it, right then, the feeling that he was doing the right thing. She was nothing close to Amy; in fact she was the complete opposite of Amy. He could hardly wait for his divorce with Amy to be finalized so that he could make Laura his new wife. But in the meantime, he would focus on spending time with her and their baby.

3 TORN: SACRIFICES OF A VAMPIRE PRINCE

"Junk, all junk." Julian Devon was channel surfing, mechanically clicking the remote, looking for something—anything—to watch. He flipped past a show he recognized and then clicked back to the channel. He'd come across a re-run of a hugely popular vampire series from a few years back. He watched the images with increasing disbelief, finally laughing out loud.

"Fantasy is right. This is about as far removed from the truth as they can get. I could make a fortune writing real-life scripts for Hollywood, instead of this drivel they pass off." Julian snapped off the television, tossing the remote on the couch. He paced back and forth in his apartment, not wanting to go out but not wanting to stay in either. He drifted to the window, looking down on the crowded New York street below. He watched the pedestrian traffic, mentally categorizing those who interested him and why, and passing over those who did not excite him at first glance.

Julian Devon was a vampire, but not an ordinary vampire. In the crowd below, he could sense individual pulses, the beating of their human hearts pumping life blood through their veins. This, to him and his clan—to any vampire for that matter, was perfectly normal.

However, what made Julian unique from most vampires was his ability to move about in the daylight. His clan, the Melosy, had developed over the millennia a certain resistance to the effects of sunlight; they could move about in the daylight with little ill effect. They could not tolerate the brightest sun on a cloudless day without some shade, but this development served them well.

No one in the clan really knew the how's or why's of this ability; legends passed down over time told of werewolves in the bloodline or of a curse that had gone wrong, none of which could be proved. But no one in the clan needed to pinpoint what allowed them to move about in the daylight. They had made it their source of strength and power.

As the next heir to the Melosy throne, Julian was well aware of that power coursing through his veins, and he was anxious to put it to use. But the current leader of the Melosy clan was his uncle, Samuel, who had no desire, or need, to step down. Samuel told Julian his age and lack of experience was keeping him from being ready to assume control of the clan any time soon. Julian chafed at the restrictions he found himself under and longed to escape, to get away until it was his turn to lead the clan.

From the street below, something suddenly caught Julian's attention, something elusive in the mix of that humanity that grabbed his senses and captivated him. There was some person, a woman—one singular woman—in the crowd whose very life essence called to him.

He closed his eyes and let his mind open completely to the sensations he was feeling, trying to locate the source of this rush that filled his body and mind. He felt his mind flow to the street, brushing against the subconscious of the people on the sidewalk as he searched for this elusive being. In some of the minds, he touched he could feel disgust at his presence, attraction in others. Some were completely blocked to him, and some were shocking in their revelations. But he didn't want to linger on those he was not interested in, not tonight.

The scent grew stronger; he was very close. He allowed his body to catch up to his mind and found himself materializing behind a slender young woman with long straight blond hair. She was dressed conservatively, just a simple coat over her dress, with bare legs and flat shoes. Nothing at all about her would draw anyone's attention, least of all Julian. But he sensed there was an inner fire burning here, and he wanted to find that fire, to play with it, allow it to singe his senses.

Julian had the ability to read people's thoughts, and as much as he wanted to know who this entrancing creature was, he hesitated. He wanted to prolong the sense of adventure, the sense of newness, and discovery he felt now.

The woman continued down the sidewalk, Julian a few paces behind her, trying to decide when and how to make his presence known. Most women practically threw themselves at Julian; one look from his flashing blue eyes or a charming smile brought them flocking to him. But this woman seemed unaware of him.

He walked a bit faster, catching up to her and casually bumping her shoulder as he passed, catching her elbow in his hand. “Oh, sorry. How clumsy of me. Are you all right?” He looked directly down into her eyes, catching his breath at their color. They were a deep green with a ring of gold around the pupil. He’d been with many, many women over the centuries, but he’d never been so captivated by just looking into a woman’s eyes. Julian was uncharacteristically at a loss for words.

“It’s okay. I’m fine.” The woman spoke, looking up at Julian. They stood for a moment on the sidewalk, he holding her arm, she looking up at him. They were being bumped and jostled by other pedestrians; Julian took the opportunity to plant a gentle suggestion in her mind, speaking the words at the same time. He wasn’t above manipulating her thoughts to his own end, but he didn’t want to learn anything else about her by reading her mind.

“Let me buy you a cup of coffee, for being so clumsy.” He gently led her to a coffee shop a few doors down from where they were standing. Julian escorted her to a booth near the back of the shop. "This is much better."

The woman looked across the table at Julian, into the bluest eyes she'd ever seen. She'd never felt such an instant attraction to a total stranger. Her arm felt tingly and electric where he'd touched her; she rubbed the spot absently with her other hand. But it also carried the tiniest bit of discomfort, almost like being stung by a bee.

"May I ask your name?" Julian's voice was soft; the woman couldn't tell if she was actually hearing him speak or just imagining the words forming in her mind. There was a rush of noise in her head, even though the coffee shop was nearly empty.

"Francesca DeVino," Her voice sounded far away. The waitress appeared and took her order. Watching her walk away, Francesca shook her head. She couldn't remember what she'd just ordered. Her mind was playing tricks on her, she thought; bits of time seemed to be disappearing. Maybe she was getting sick.

Julian watched the woman carefully. He'd discovered over the centuries that some mortals were far more sensitive to having their minds touched by his than others. This woman, Francesca, seemed particularly sensitive. He pulled back from her mind, allowing her to center herself, to gather her thoughts. He watched the slight puzzled frown that had been creasing her forehead disappear. He'd have to be very gentle with this woman. The thought was strangely exciting.

"I'm sorry. I was a bit distracted. My name is Francesca DeVino. What's your name? I don't think I caught it." Francesca wasn't even sure he'd told her his name. Her head was clearing, the rushing sounds were fading. The world suddenly seemed to snap back into focus.

"Julian Devon. It's a pleasure to meet you, Francesca, even if it's because I'm such a klutz. You're not hurt, are you?" He nodded toward her arm. The waitress arrived with her coffee.

"Oh, no, I'm fine." She realized she was still rubbing her arm, not where he'd bumped her but from where he'd taken hold to guide her here. She made a fuss over adding cream and sugar to her coffee, relieved to see she had ordered just a black coffee.

They spent the next half hour in easy conversation. Julian learned that Francesca was an editor at a publishing company, that her work was interesting but occasionally tedious. She lived around the corner from Julian. He wondered how he could have missed her all the times she'd walked past his apartment. Maybe, he wasn't as observant as he thought he was.

Julian realized he was mesmerized by almost everything Francesca said. He wanted her like he'd never wanted any woman before. She was beautiful, alluring, intelligent, and arousing; she was, to him, the perfect woman.

It was growing dark when Julian suggested she might like to come back to his apartment for a drink before dinner. Francesca's initial response was to say no; Julian gently planted the suggestion that she say yes. They walked the few blocks to Julian's apartment in the fading light of the day.

Julian's apartment was dark as they entered; he was reluctant to turn on any lights, letting the filtered glow from outside light of the apartment. After taking her coat and purse, he gently reached for her, pulling her against him. He felt Francesca tense against him for a moment as he held her. He wanted to enter her subconscious, to tell her not to be afraid, but he didn't want to overwhelm her sensitive mind by intruding too far.

With the gentlest of pressure, he sent his thoughts to her, gossamer feelings of acceptance. He wanted her to experience her own feelings as he made love to her; he didn't want to control her any more than necessary. But he wanted her at ease in her mind before they moved any further physically. He was relieved when he felt her body relax in his arms, and he pulled his mind back from hers.

Francesca suddenly, inexplicably, felt her initial resistance to Julian's advances fade. She had never had a one-night stand; she'd never even had more than just a few unsatisfactory relationships over the past few years. This was all new to her and had felt all wrong just a moment ago; only cheap women had sex with men they'd just met. But a thought had suddenly washed over her mind that this was going to be okay, that there was nothing to fear in being with Julian; he had only her best interests at heart. Her body followed her mind's lead, and she felt herself melting into Julian's embrace.

With the last barrier in Francesca's mind dissolved, Julian pulled her against his body. He bent his head and kissed her neck, running his tongue over the soft skin, tracing the lines of the veins he could feel there. He could sense her life blood running beneath the fragile skin and his latent desire to taste that blood ran as a not-so-subtle undercurrent to his more overwhelming sexual desires. Julian could successfully restrain his need to feed on blood, but he did need to control his desire to bite during sex. The two, for him, were so intimately intertwined; the desire to become one not only during the act of making love, but becoming one by tasting a mortal's life force… or another vampire, if they engaged in play biting during sex. He pushed his desires for her blood aside and concentrated on the purely physical pleasures of making love to this beautiful woman.

Francesca felt the first stirrings of sexual desire deep within her body. As Julian's tongue travelled over her neck, her breathing quickened and she pushed her body against him. She ran her hands up the front of Julian's shirt, wrapping her arms around his neck. She turned her head, seeking his mouth with hers.

Julian responded by kissing her, running his tongue over her lips, teasing her for a moment. He gently captured her bottom lip with his teeth, exerting just enough pressure to bring him to the edge of piercing her flesh. He felt her gasp and released her lip, chided himself for almost losing control. He resumed kissing her, probing her lips with his, forcing her mouth open with his tongue.

Francesca responded to the increased pressure of Julian's kiss, opening her mouth to him and letting his tongue play with hers. The contact between them was sending electric sparks through her. She began moving her body against Julian, longing for more contact between them, her breasts growing heavy with desire, her nipples becoming sensitive to every brush against the fabric of her clothes.

Julian slid his hands down her shoulders, finding her breasts pressed between their bodies, and began gently massaging them, hearing Francesca's sharp intake of breath. Her breasts were full in his hands, and he could feel the nipples grow hard beneath his fingers. He looked down into her eyes, watching them darken with passion as he increased the pressure on those breasts, now kneading them together, hearing her moan softly.

He wondered how much sexual experience Francesca had, but resisted entering her mind to find out. He wanted to experience the surprise of discovering what turned her on, what made her hot. The thought that he might be the first man to ever stir these feelings in her had a profound physical effect on him. He felt his body respond, felt his cock grow hard, pulling the fabric of his pants tight.

His hands found the buttons on Francesca's blouse and undid them, the garment opening, revealing two full mounds barely contained within the lacy fabric of a half bra. He was momentarily startled by such an arousing garment: the black lace was transparent, the nipples and areola clearly visible. He was struck by the contrast of this demure girl wearing such a sexy bra; it excited him, made him wonder what other secrets she held.

Francesca watched Julian bend to kiss her exposed breasts. His lips were hot on her skin as she wound her fingers through his thick, dark hair, cradling him to her as he kissed a soft line down one breast to the top edge of her bra. She watched as he kissed one nipple through the fabric of the bra, flicking it lightly with his tongue, and then moving to the other. Heat flood through her then, beginning in the pit of her stomach and sending warmth throughout her entire body, something she'd never experienced before, but thoroughly enjoyed.

Julian kissed and licked Francesca's hard nipples through the thin lace of her bra, the fabric growing wet. He pulled the top of her bra down roughly, exposing the rose-colored nipples, sucking on one, pulling it further into his mouth, rolling the nipple with his tongue, nibbling at it with his teeth, feeling Francesca shudder in pleasure. He looked up at her then, watching him suckle her breast and felt his cock growing harder. Moving to the other breast, he took that nipple into his mouth, sucking harder this time, feeding his own arousal grow along with Francesca's.

Driven wild by Julian's mouth and hands, Francesca looked down at him sucking on her breasts. Watching him was as exciting as the sensations his tongue and teeth were creating. She wanted more though, suddenly wanted to feel him naked against her. Pulling his head away from her breast, she sought his mouth with hers, reaching for his erection at the same time. She felt how hard he was, and rubbed the length of his cock with her hand through his pants. He responded to her touch with a groan, thrusting his cock against her hand. Francesca found the snap and zipper on his pants, quickly undoing them, tugging his pants and boxers down over his hips as Julian stripped his shirt over his head.

As his cock sprang free, Julian heard Francesca gasp. He looked down at her, watching the emotions play across her face. He wanted to enter her mind, to experience what she was experiencing, but held himself back, not wanting to overwhelm her mind with his; he was very aroused to watch as she apparently admired what she saw. He watched her rub his cock with her delicate hand, tentative at first but gaining confidence.

This was all new territory for Francesca. As she held his cock uncertainly in her hand, Julian began moving his hips, and she quickly caught on to what he wanted, stroking his cock with more force, picking up the rhythm of his movement. She'd never been with a man who had taken any time with foreplay. Her last boyfriend had considered a kiss good enough; she'd never had the chance to explore a man's body, much less explore one who apparently enjoyed it so much and encouraged her.

He kissed her deeply then, driving all other thoughts from her mind, thrusting his tongue into her mouth, holding her breasts in his hands, feverishly rubbing the still-wet nipples with his thumbs. He slid one hand down her back, finding the zipper of her skirt and sliding it down, pulling her skirt off and letting it fall to the floor. One hand slid down beneath the waistband of her panties, sliding a finger into her slit, feeling how wet she was. She moved beneath him, giving him more access to her clit. He rubbed that mound of flesh for a moment, feeling it grow hard beneath his fingers, as they grew wet with her juices. His desire for her at that moment was more than he'd ever felt for any woman.

Francesca gasped as Julian swept her up, carrying her easily down the hall to his bedroom. He laid her gently on the bed.

"God, you're beautiful," he breathed, looking down with hooded eyes at her. Her breasts were round and firm, still barely contained by her bra. Her waist was narrow above full hips. She was wearing a pair of black silk panties, plain but extremely sexy. He realized he'd never really enjoyed the simple pleasures of just looking at a mortal woman without wanting to taste her blood; he'd found it was easier so far to control his desire to bite Francesca, to taste her life blood, than he'd originally thought. He was rather pleased with his restraint so far. But he wasn't sure how long he could resist.

Francesca blushed under Julian's gaze, but was aroused at being the center of Julian's attention. As he stood at the side of the bed watching, she sat up and unhooked her bra, discarding the garment. She felt Julian's eyes on her breasts, felt him drinking her in, and it gave her a sense of feminine power. Reaching out, she stroked his hard cock, running her fingers down its length, over his balls and back up over the crown, rubbing her thumb over the sensitive tip. Julian shuddered, his cock twitching in her hand, growing harder at her touch.

Julian let her stroke his cock for a moment, growing harder at her touch than he could have ever imagined. He needed her to stop though before he came, just at her touch. Placing his hand over hers, he gently stopped her. He reached down then to pull her panties over her hips and legs. He moved over her on the bed, gently spreading her legs, running his hands gently up and down the insides of her thighs, kneeling between her legs for a moment. He saw raw passion in her eyes and sensed she was ready for him. He brushed his mind briefly against hers, intending to relax her if she was afraid, but he found she was eagerly anticipating sex. In fact, he was surprised by her thoughts; they were far from demure or ladylike.

Julian placed his hands on the bed on either side of Francesca's shoulders. "Are you ready for me? Do you want me to fuck you now, Francesca?" Julian growled out the words, looking into her eyes, wanting her to say the words he heard in her mind. He was not disappointed.

"Yes, Julian, fuck me... fuck me hard. I want your cock inside me." Francesca had never said those words before, although she had longed to say them to Julian. She felt a rush at being able to say those words out loud.

Julian bent down and kissed her roughly, grinding her lips against his. He felt Francesca slide her legs up his body, locking them around his waist, pulling his body toward hers. He reached between them, guiding his rock hard cock into her waiting wet pussy. He felt the tip of his cock enter Francesca, felt her warmth and wetness. He paused for the briefest moment and then thrust hard into her, filling all of her with his cock. He felt her roll her hips to meet his thrust, feel her opening up even more of herself to him. He pulled back, holding his body above her and then thrust back, hard, into that waiting pussy.

Francesca matched him then, stroke for stroke, as Julian thrust his hard cock into that pussy, pounding himself over and over into Francesca. He could feel her breath coming in short gasps, could feel her movements beneath him becoming faster. He wanted to watch her face as he worked his cock into her, wanted to see her emotions as she climaxed.

Francesca had never experienced sex like this. She found herself quickly at the edge of an orgasm. She felt her body begin to lose control; her movements become almost frantic as she sought release.

Julian pulled back then, holding himself above her, teasing her, rubbing the tip of his cock against her clit. “Make me come, Julian, please bring me off." The sound of her voice combined with her words sent him over the edge. He thrust himself into her hard, felt her respond instantly, bracing her feet on the bed and bucking up against him. He watched as she threw her head back, eyes closed, lips parted, her hands racking across his back. She arched sharply against him as waves of pleasure coursed through her body. He could feel her pussy contracting around his cock.

Julian buried his face in Francesca's neck as he felt her orgasm flood through her; he felt his fangs graze her jugular vein as his own orgasm began to build. The heat in his balls was intense, pushing up the shaft of his cock, bursting out of him as he thrust into Francesca with rough cry. At the moment of his own release, he longed to sink his fangs into her neck, to feel the sweet taste of her life blood on his tongue, to make his orgasm complete. But he held back, his cock continuing to pump his cum into her wet pussy.

They lay in each other's arms as their orgasms faded, talking in soft voices. Julian held Francesca as she drifted off to sleep. He lay awake for several hours, watching her sleep, still amazed that he had found her.

They became almost inseparable over the next few weeks. Francesca began stopping by Julian's apartment after work almost every day, spending the night in Julian's big bed, having delicious love made to her and learning how to please him in ways she'd never imagined.

Julian realized he'd fallen deeply in love

with Francesca, something he had never thought possible. He'd known women over the centuries, but he'd never felt this attached to any one woman. To imagine someone he could spend eternity with was more than he'd ever imagined. But for that to happen, he'd have to turn her, to make her like him, to work the dark trick. That was something serious, not something to take lightly. And to be perfectly fair to Francesca, he should ask her permission. But how could he do that if he hadn't even told her what he was.

Francesca had appeared at his door one evening in tears. When she had calmed down, she told him that her grandmother had died. The old woman had been sick for many years so even though the death was not unexpected; Francesca was very upset. She stayed with Julian that night, neither of them getting much sleep. While Francesca was distraught over her grandmother's death, Julian was upset for a different reason.

Even though Julian knew it intellectually, it struck him with almost physical force that Francesca could die and it could happen any day. She could be in an accident, there could be a fire; she could become ill and die. He was panicked at the thought of her leaving his apartment before he could turn her and he almost bit her right then and there. But his conscience would not allow him to do that before he had a chance to tell her what he was and what he intended to do to her. It never occurred to him she would object.

Francesca had finally fallen asleep in his arms, wearing one of his old T-shirts. He'd stripped down to his boxers and relaxed against the pillows, exhausted himself. Even though he could be about in the sunlight, he still needed rest like any other being. He dozed off, dreaming he was making love to Francesca.

In his dream, they were on the bed, he reclines, and Francesca, wearing his shirt, was straddling him, riding his erect cock. He was cupping her ass with both hands, spreading her ass cheeks as he drove himself upwards into her sweet pussy. She had one breast in her hand, holding it for Julian as he sucked on the hard nipple. He looked up at Francesca, and saw the passion in her eyes. "I'm coming, Julian... suck me harder, suck my tits harder."

In his dream, he sucked on her harder, feeling his fangs graze her breast, feeling blood in his mouth. He could hear Francesca's voice urging him to suck harder, and he did, feeling her life's blood running down his throat. Francesca screamed in pleasure.

Francesca's scream of pain jolted him awake, his face buried in her neck, feeling her blood on his lips, tasting it in his mouth. He pulled back in horror, looking down at what he'd done at her, blood running down from two puncture wounds in her neck.

He'd bitten her, bitten Francesca. It was too late to take back what he'd done; even if he didn't drink anymore, she'd die. If he did drink more, she would surely die. All he could do now was to feed her his blood, to turn her into a vampire or risk losing her forever.

He quickly opened a vein on his wrist with

a quick slash against a fang, holding his arm to her mouth. His blood trickled between her lips, and he watched anxiously as she swallowed, first slowly and then with increasing speed. He let her feed for a few moments and then eased her back on the pillows. He left her for a moment, returning with a damp towel, wiping away the smears of blood from Francesca's neck and face.

Julian's emotions were torn. He truly regretted biting Francesca, even in a dream-state, even accidentally. He had no idea how to tell her what had happened. But a tiny part of him, a part that was growing, was pleased. Francesca was now his forever. He lay back down beside her, curling her against his body. Newly made vampires usually slept for several hours; he anticipated Francesca would be asleep well into the next day, he hoped past sunset. He wasn't sure if she would inherit his ability to withstand sunlight, but he didn't want to take any chances.

Movement on the bed jarred Julian awake. Francesca was getting up, moving sluggishly, looking dazed. She tried to stand but lost her balance and fell back on the bed.

"Julian, I don't feel well." Francesca sat on the edge of the bed, shaky and pale.

"I know, I know you feel bad. But you're not sick. Listen, there's something I have to tell you. You'll need to listen carefully to me. Can you listen to me, Francesca?" Julian knelt down in front of her, taking her hands in his.

"Sure. Is it about my grandmother?" Francesca's voice sounded tired and weak.

"No, sweetie, it's not about her. It's about

you, and me. About us." He took a deep breath. "You and I are alike now. We're both vampires. I have turned you into a vampire, like me." Julian wasn't sure this was exactly the best way to explain this but he forged ahead. Francesca didn't look like she quite understood what he was explaining.

"You know there are things about me that seem... different. We've never eaten a meal together. You either eat before we go out or I tell you I'm not hungry, I've already eaten. That's because vampires don't eat food; we don't need to eat. We drink blood." He saw Francesca recoil a bit at the word blood; he also saw a dawning awareness in her eyes.

"You'll be fine now, you're safe with me. I'll help you adjust, teach you what you need to know. I'll feed you; you won't need to hunt. None of us hunt anymore, or at least we don't need to hunt. There is synthetic blood for us..." Julian decided he'd tell her later it tasted horrid. "But I'm always here for you. Always. We'll be together forever."

Francesca looked at him with glazed eyes. "I'm hungry. I want to eat." She tried again to stand but Julian gently held her down.

"Here." He brought his wrist to his mouth and opened a vein with a fang. He held his arm to Francesca's mouth. She looked at him with a puzzled look, not understanding. "Drink, Francesca. Drink my blood; it will feed you."

Francesca held his wrist to her mouth. He could feel her slowly sucking on his wrist, feel his blood flowing into her body. As she grew stronger, she began sucking harder on his wrist. He saw the glazed look leave her eyes and a rosy flush creep up her face.

She was sucking greedily now, and Julian had to gently pry her mouth from his wrist. She tried to grab for his arm, but he held her back. She wiped her mouth with the back of her hand, no longer looking weak or dazed. There was a fire in her eyes Julian had never seen before.

"How do you feel?" he asked. Francesca tried to stand again, finding her balance as Julian held her arm. She took a few hesitant steps.

"I feel better," she said. Francesca took a few steps away from him. "In fact, I feel wonderful." She spun around, turning to face Julian. The fire in her eyes blazed now. "I've never felt this full of energy or life before. You're telling me you've done this to me? That you've turned me into a vampire?" Her voice had taken on a sharper tone than he was used to. He thought it was a temporary effect, something that would change as her body became used to its new state of being.

Francesca had never felt such a surge of energy; her whole being throbbed with electricity. She felt as if she could run for miles or have sex for days; she could hear things from down the block. She turned back to Julian, who was looking at her with a puzzled frown. She strode toward him, pushing him down on the bed.

"Make love to me, Julian. I want to feel you inside of me now." She pulled the T-shirt over her head. She reached down and pulled off Julian's boxers, taking his cock roughly in her hand. She began stroking him until he was erect in her hand. She straddled him then, guiding his cock into her pussy, settling her weight on his cock.

Julian was amazed at the change in Francesca. She'd grown more assertive over their weeks together, but this aggressive woman was totally foreign to him. His body responded to her; he was powerless not to.

He grabbed her hips as she began riding his cock up and down, her hands holding him flat on the bed, her breasts above his face. He tried to keep up with her, but she suddenly seemed possessed. He let her take control, swept along in her frantic pace.

Within minutes, Francesca was on the verge of orgasm. She threw her head back, a hoarse cry tearing from her throat. Julian could do nothing but watch in amazement as Francesca's orgasm tore through her, as her body bucked and twisted against him. As her orgasm faded, she looked down at Julian. He was shocked to see her eyes had changed from their beautiful green to a deadly flat black. He was used to seeing vampire eyes change to brilliant red as they were caught in the lust of feeding, but he'd never seen any vampire with black eyes.

Francesca rolled off of Julian, panting from exertion. Before he could say anything, she left his bedroom. Moments later, he heard the front door of his apartment close. She'd left.

It was several days before Julian saw Francesca again. She's stopped going to work, stopped answering her phone. He had been worried sick but hadn't been able to track her down. He'd gone out as often as he could, drifting over the city, trying to catch her scent in the crowds. He'd asked among clan members if they'd seen her or heard of her.

The only information he got back were reports of several unusual and bloody murders that had occurred in the city within the past three days. The clan had warned him to be on his guard at all times; no one knew the identity of the victims but all had been bled dry. It appeared as though the murders had been committed by a rogue vampire.

While horrified at the murders, Julian was relieved none of the victims was Francesca. He continued to search for her scent; even a molecule on the wind could lead him to her.

He was drifting through the city almost a week after he'd turned Francesca when he caught her scent. Sending his mind out to her, he found her in an alley behind a dive bar. He watched her from a distance, materializing on a fire escape a short way away. She was with a drunk from the bar, a drunk who had her pinned against the wall, her skirt pushed up around her hips as he groped beneath it, ramming his fingers into her panties.

Francesca reached down and grabbed the man's crotch, making him grunt and rub against her. As his head fell on her shoulder, he saw Francesca tilt her head down and sink her fangs into the man's neck. Julian watched in horror as she tore out man's neck, the blood spurting from his severed vessels, spraying over Francesca's face and chest. She gulped at the blood as it poured from him.

Julian could hear the terrible noises she made as she drank in his blood.

When she was finished, when there was apparently no blood left in his body, she casually tossed him aside. The man fell in a crumpled, boneless heap next to a dumpster. As Julian watched, Francesca wiped her mouth with the back of her hand. As Julian moved away from the wall, she glanced up and saw him. She snarled, pulling her lips back from her bloody fangs in a feral grimace. Julian had never been afraid of anything but seeing the woman he loved... had loved... look at him with such hatred chilled him to the very core.

He knew then who had committed the other murders; it was Francesca. With a heavy heart, he realized it would be he who would have to put her down. He was responsible for this vampire he created, and it was his responsibility to keep her from killing senselessly. It went against every rule of the clan; mortals were not to be killed for sport or as vengeance or retaliation. And if another clan member discovered what he'd done, who'd he created... what she'd done... and that he'd not done anything to stop her, he would be made to leave the clan. And that could not happen, not to him.

Descending down to where Francesca stood, still snarling at him, he moved toward her, watching her every move. The same deadly black eyes he'd been in her face before glared at him with unconcealed hatred. He had no idea how strong she would be, but he was confident he was faster than she was.

With one swift movement, he reached out and grabbed her throat, tearing flesh, feeling her hot blood running between his fingers. At that moment, Julian tried to erase all the love he felt for Francesca. She struggled in his grip, clawing at his hands, but was no match for his strength. Julian continued to hold her by the throat as her struggles weakened, eventually ceasing. She was finally still. Julian let her body slide to the ground.

Francesca's death—her death by his own hands—devastated Julian. He felt as if his own heart had been torn out. He'd killed for food, of course, but only out of necessity, before he'd learned to feed from his victim, leaving them alive, rather than kill them. For him, New York was now haunted by her presence; he swore he could smell her scent everywhere. Staying in his apartment was out of the question; he'd moved into a hotel, which did not suit him at all. This had been the woman he wanted to spend eternity with; he doubted now if he could ever find anyone who he could love, who would excite him on so many levels. He wasn't sure he wanted to look again. It had taken him centuries to find Francesca and that had been a complete accident. He resigned himself to a life without companionship.

Julian was torn about telling his Uncle Samuel what had happened. Once he'd located Francesca—once the killings had stopped—he had not gone back to Samuel to explain it was Francesca, or how she came to be a vampire. The confusion and shame he felt for creating such a vicious creature weighed heavily on him.

Samuel had been his mentor most of his life; Julian's father, Eric, was cold and distant, even for a vampire. They had never connected in the way he did with Samuel. Julian suspected some long-simmering dispute between the two of them; it was logical that Eric would one day assume control of the Melosy, but instead, it was Julian who was slated to be the next to inherit the clan.

Not knowing what else to do, Julian decided to leave the country, to put as much distance as he could between New York and himself. Over the decades, he'd met other Melosy from other countries, including Sweden. With its long dark winter nights, Sweden was a comfortable country for many vampiric clans, not just the Melosy. Those without the Melosy genes had many more hours of night during the long Scandinavian winters in which to move about—to hunt and feed.

He made contact with other vampires in Sweden, and they arranged for a small apartment for him in Stockholm. It was mid-December when he left New York. He took a longer flight from to Stockholm, with a several hour layover in Paris; he had always enjoyed Paris. He found a very charming, and willing, young woman who satisfied his needs, both for nourishment and for sex. Her blood was as rich and heady as any fine wine found in the city. He savored every drop he drank, and every moment he spent with her, sending her on her way, almost as satisfied as he was. But she was just a girl in Paris on his layover; he hadn't even bothered to ask her name.

The flight arrived in Stockholm in the early evening; it had been dark for several hours. He took a taxi from the airport to his apartment. After unpacking, he went for a walk in the cold night air. Stockholm was decorated for the upcoming holiday season; the entire city seemed to glow with white lights. Julian barely noticed.

He was looking in shop windows, idly thinking about buying a pair of gloves. Vampires were not affected by cold, but he liked to give the appearance he was mortal; in Stockholm in December, everyone was wearing gloves. After unpacking, he realized he'd either forgotten or lost the one pair he owned.

"Looking for something special?" Julian felt someone at his elbow, a low voice in his ear. The language was English; the accent was Swedish. He turned, obviously expecting to see someone female, but was momentarily speechless at the beautiful woman standing next to him.

"Yes. I am." Julian sounded abrupt, even to himself, but he was still stunned by the woman standing before him. She was nearly as tall as he was, with classic Scandinavian features; high cheek bones, a fine straight nose and large blue eyes, her face framed by blonde hair. Julian felt a stirring deep inside, purely sexual, but still a stirring. His senses went on alert. She was also impeccably dressed, something Julian responded to.

"Are you new to Stockholm? I see you are missing your gloves." The woman held up one elegantly gloved hand before him. "Your fingers must be cold."

Julian made the decision that he wanted to spend some time with this woman. She might be an interesting diversion while he was in Sweden. She was confident, something he appreciated, possibly cultured. He was in no way interested in anything long term, but he always enjoyed the company of beautiful women. And he had desires that needed attention. This woman seemed to fit all his requirements for a light entertaining relationship.

He tried sending a mental suggestion to her that she suggest they go for a drink, but before he even fully formed the idea, she interrupted his thoughts.

"Would you like to get a drink? I know a nice little place not far from here. We can discuss the best types of gloves you might need here in chilly Stockholm," she smiled at him, her gaze direct.

They spent the evening in a small cozy bar. Julian learned her name was Alia; she was a gallery owner, displaying contemporary paintings and sculpture. Julian discovered she was extremely intelligent and very well-read. They discussed books they'd both read, talked about movies they'd seen. She seemed to have read or seen almost everything Julian had; he found it infinitely refreshing to have an intelligent conversation with someone, someone as beautiful as Alia.

Julian was prepared to plant the suggestion they retire to his apartment; he found he was as attracted to Alia's body as he was her mind. He was beginning to feel the first stirs of desire; Alia had the habit of lightly touching his hand as she spoke and each touch left a lingering electric current running through him. At one point, during the evening, he found his mind wandering, imagining what she would look like undressed; if her body was as beautiful as her face, what it would be like to spend an entire night exploring that body, if she was as assertive in bed as she was outside of it.

With a start, he realized she'd asked him a question. "You're a million miles away, Julian. Were you having a nice little daydream?" She smiled at him. "I asked if you'd like to come back to my apartment with me. I'm just around the corner."

She seemed to have the uncanny ability to read his mind. He was slightly alarmed by this but also pleased she was taking the initiative. They left the bar, walking arm and arm a short distance to her apartment.

Alia's apartment was high up in an older building, with elegant high ceilings and carved moldings, very old world. In sharp contrast, she had on display many modern pieces of sculpture and other artwork; Julian assumed they were from her gallery. The combination should have been jarring, but she had artfully married the two diverse styles.

"I'm going to change into something a little more comfortable, to quote an old movie cliché. Help yourself to whatever you'd like from the bar." Julian watched her walk down the long hallway, disappearing behind a tall ivory-painted door. He felt a subtle movement in his cock; watching her walk away had revived his earlier daydream. She had a luscious-looking ass beneath her long tight skirt; he had the most overwhelming desire to stand behind her, grab her hips and rub himself against her, feeling what he imagined to be a firm, yet giving, pair of ass cheeks. He felt his erection growing, a bulge beginning to show at the front of his pants. He'd have to control himself a little better, unless he misread her signals entirely. But he didn't think he was.

Alia returned, in a blood-red satin robe, the sash neatly tied at her narrow waist, her early suit jacket and skirt gone. She looked more relaxed and obviously very much at ease with him. She moved past him to the bar, pouring herself a glass of wine. He noticed with a deep sense of arousal that she'd also discarded her bra; the sway of her breasts as she poured the wine could only mean they were just there, on the other side of a thin layer of satin. His cock took notice, rising again, against his will. Julian turned away from her, to look out the full-length windows; the view was spectacular.

"The view is beautiful at night." Alia moved to stand beside him, leaning her head on his shoulder. He could smell the perfume of her hair; feel the warmth of her, the warmth of the blood coursing through her veins. He sensed her heartbeat; it was beating fast.

Alia took a sip of wine and set the glass down. She turned to face him. "I think we both know where this is headed, don't we? I believe in being honest and straightforward. I want you to make love to me, Julian. You, I believe, want the same." She glanced down, arching an eyebrow, smiling at the evidence of his arousal; his erection was again making a very noticeable bulge in his pants.

Julian was momentarily disarmed by her assertiveness; but he realized he was actually relieved to find a woman he didn't need to seduce, who went after what she wanted. She was much like him; when he wanted a woman, he went after her. Apparently, Alia knew what she wanted and it was him.

But he was not going to be passive by any means; Julian took one step toward Alia and ran his hands up her satin-covered arms, pulling her against him. He kissed her, gently at first, tasting the wine on her lips. Alia's lips parted, her tongue dancing across his lips. He deepened their kiss, exploring her mouth with his tongue, feeling her give back equal pressure.

But kissing her was not going to be enough, not matter how sensual it was. As Alia wrapped her arms around his neck, Julian slid his hands down to her waist, amazingly tiny above the flair of her hips. The sash of her robe was tied loosely; with a gentle tug the robe fell open. Julian slid his hands inside, running them up to cup her breasts, round and firm in his hands. He gently fondled them, skating his thumbs over the nipples, feeling them harden at his touch; he felt more than heard Alia moan softly. Julian could feel her heart, almost see it beating beneath her breasts. It was a very strong heart, pumping rich blood through her body.

The urge to bite almost overcame him, swift and powerful in its intensity. He grunted as the sensation flooded through him, crushing her breasts with his hands, grinding his mouth down on Alia's. He felt is erection growing even more, becoming even more engorged, even larger. She startled beneath him; he tore his mouth from hers, turning his head away. He longed to sink his fangs into her breasts, feel her blood wash over him, swallow until he was sated. Willing himself under control, breathing heavily, he forced down inside himself the base desire to feed on this woman.

Alia's hand on his throbbing erection brought him back to the present; at least, it focused his attention on something other than feeding. Her hand was warm as she rubbed the entire length of his cock, sliding her fingers between his legs, massaging his balls and the base of his cock. Julian closed his eyes, groaning against her neck, all his senses focused on her hand groping him. He tilted his hips forward, seeking more contact.

He felt the zipper on his pants slide down; his raging erection thrusting out at Alia as she expertly pulled down his pants. She took him back into her soft hand, stroking the length of him. He looked down at his cock in her hand, watched her stroking him. The sight of his cock being worked by a woman always fueled his passion; while watching Alia this feeling was magnified. She stroked him harder, watching his face as she jacked his cock with her hand.

The robe fell to the floor as he slid it from her shoulders, exposing her porcelain skin, her breasts now visible to him. Her nipples were hard, her breasts full with her desire, right there, ready for his hands and mouth. Suddenly, he overcame with the need to feel her breasts in his mouth, to suck and kiss and lick them.

Working at her breast almost frantically, he licked the nipple, pulling it into his mouth, sucking hard as he groped the other tit with his hand. It was like dying of thirst and finding the source of all water; he felt he couldn't get enough of her breast in his mouth. He was thrusting his cock into Alia's hand; she responded by grabbing his throbbing erection with both hands, twisting them in opposite directions around the shaft of his cock.

Julian slid one hand down between Alia's legs, feeling the heat of her pussy. She spread her legs, allowing him full access. His fingers slid into her pussy, thrusting into her, making her gasp. She pushed her hips forward as Julian continued working his fingers deeper, pushing into her, stroking her inside. Her stomach muscles contracted involuntarily, almost bending her double as Julian's fingers found some secret trigger in her pussy. She felt liquid squirt from her, felt it running down her legs. She was crying out with each thrust of his hand, each time feeling like its own orgasm. The feelings were almost too intense; she wanted him to stop but she wanted desperately to feel more.

They were panting against each other; Julian thrusting his hand into Alia's pussy, she working his cock with both hands. They were both crying out, Julian's grunts were muffled against Alia's breast as he still sucked on her tit. Alia's cries were getting sharper, higher pitched. Julian sensed she was being driven over the edge. He suddenly wanted his cock in her pussy instead of his fingers, wanted to fuck her, fuck her until she screamed, bringing her to orgasm.

Julian left Alia's breast, the nipple and breast wet. He stood up, lifted her off the floor and carried her to the rug in front of the fire. He laid her on her back, her pussy glistening wet, her legs coated with her rich juices. She looked amazingly beautiful in the light of the fire; her eyes were dark with passion, the fire making her skin glow.

"Fuck me, Julian, fuck me please. Make me come." She was practically begging. Julian lowered himself between her legs, aching to bury his cock in her pussy. This wasn't the time for creative positions or gentle exploration; this was the time for him to pound her pussy, sending them both over the edge.

Alia spread her legs as Julian guided his thick hard cock into her with one hand, touching the tip to her clit for just a second, holding there, looking into her eyes. She was biting her lower lip; she nodded at him.

With one thrust, he buried himself in Alia's pussy. She cried out beneath him, rolling her hips up and pulling her legs back. Julian placed his hands on either side of her, settling

Alia's legs on his shoulders. He pulled back slowly, held himself with just the tip of his cock in her. And then, he thrust into her again. She screamed this time, grabbing her breasts, rubbing the nipples. Watching her beneath him, watching her crush her breasts in her hands, those breasts he'd just worked with his own hands and mouth, was incredible.

Julian let loose then, pounding into her repeatedly, feeling his balls slap against her ass, driving his cock into her. She was incredibly tight, and his cock was squeezed by her pussy. The pressure was intense; he felt his balls filling with heat, his orgasm starting to build, forcing pressure up the shaft of his cock. He could feel Alia's body moving beneath him; he sent his mind to her, wanting to know how close she was. He did not want to hold back, didn't think he really could but he wanted her to come first, wanted to watch her as she came.

Alia's orgasm was closer than he realized. He pulled away from her mind, concentrating on his physical being. His cock ached to explode, and he shifted his position slightly, thrusting into Alia at a different angle. She put her hands on his shoulders, pushing him away from her, putting her feet on the bed. She pushed up against him, grinding her hips against his.

"Come on, Alia..." Julian growled, looking down at her. "Come for me." He saw a fire in her eyes, saw his words pushing her over the edge. She bucked one last time, hard, against him. He felt a gush of liquid, her pussy contracting around his cock; she screamed as her orgasm flooded through her.

"Oh, God! Julian! Pound me harder!" He couldn't imagine how he could manage that. He threw his head back, bracing his knees against the floor, driving his hips forward even harder. He couldn't hold back then, his cock wanting to explode with his hot load, to shoot into her.

He thrust into her hard—very hard—three short sharp thrusts, screaming out with each, finally letting his orgasm flood into her, buried in her as he shook, his hips continuing to push forward. Alia was shuddering beneath him, eyes closed, mouth open, each of his thrusts making her cry out. He wasn't sure if she was feeling pleasure or pain, and for a brief moment, he didn't really care. He wanted to finish his orgasm, to keep pumping until he was dry.

They finally came down from their experience. Each was panting, slick with sweat. Julian moved gently from Alia, lying down next to her, cradling her against him. The fire warmed them as they recovered. They dozed after a time, eventually making their way, tired, spent but ultimately and supremely satisfied, to Alia's bedroom. They were asleep in minutes.

Over the next few weeks, Julian spent more time with Alia, allowing her to show him Stockholm. He was reluctant to include her in every aspect of his new life though; he needed to keep a distance between him, to keep his heart from becoming involved; he was not giving his heart to any woman, even Alia.

She seemed to understand his distance, respecting when he needed to be alone. He discovered several clubs on his own, where he could find other women to satisfy his need to feed, and occasionally, his sexual needs as well. The women of Sweden were very accommodating to all of his needs and desires.

But he did treasure Alia for her intelligence; he valued her insights and opinions, looking forward to spending long evenings discussing books and movies and then longer nights in her big bed. Julian was astonished to discover Alia was a student of more adventurous sexual techniques. She continually surprised him; one night might be role-playing, another might involve handcuffs. One night included a video camera. He'd never imagined himself as the star in his own porn video, but he found it almost unbearably exciting as he first fucked Alia while watching them on the monitor, and then watched the whole experience again, as Alia expertly sucked his cock to a massive orgasm.

"Wouldn't it be wonderful to be able to watch these forever? To see how they change over the decades? I'd love to have the super power, or whatever it would be, to live forever."

Julian was quiet; he'd been thinking of telling Alia his secret, that he was a vampire. They'd discussed other things; he'd told her about Francesca, obviously leaving out crucial details about her death and his role in it, and why he killed her. And that he was a vampire.

"Look!" Alia pointed; the fireworks had started. She was like a little girl; she clapped her hands at each explosion. One particular firework struck both of them as extremely beautiful: a large brilliant ball of light exploded behind the silhouette of a leafless tree. For a moment, it looked as if the tree had come to life, not with leaves, but with fire. They were both silent for a moment.

"It looked like the tree came to life for a minute. How beautiful." Alia looked up at Julian. "Don't you agree?" Julian leaned down, kissing her cold lips.

"Do you really want to live forever?" They were back in Alia's warm apartment, Julian lighting a fire, talking over his shoulder. Alia was curled on the couch. Julian sat beside her, tucking her hair behind her ear. "If you could, I mean?" Julian looked closely at Alia, waiting for her answer.

"Yes, I think I would. I've thought about it for a long time. You know, there are some beings that are immortal. Fairies and elves, vampires... all those creatures of myths and legends." Alia got a faraway look in her eyes. "It would be amazing, I think."

"Wouldn't you miss people here, those you love, your family?" Julian probed deeper, looking for answers.

"I have no family. I've never been married. I have no children. Who would I miss?" Alia was matter of fact in her list. "I'm living a great life; I could continue living a great life for a very, very long time."

"But why? Why do you want to live forever?" Julian held her hand, stroking her fingers.

She shifted uncomfortably on the couch. "I've never really told anyone this. But truly, I fear death. I am terrified of dying. I think sometimes I'd do almost anything to keep living forever."

Julian took a deep breath. "Alia, I have something to tell you. I think I can make your wish come true." Alia looked at him, a puzzled frown on her face.

"Can you work miracles?" She laughed lightly at him. "Or do you do magic?" When he didn't smile back, or answer, she grew serious.

"What can you do, Julian? How can you make my wish come true?"

"I am a vampire," he'd never said those words before. It took all his courage to continue. He repeated: "I am a vampire. I can make you a vampire. It's not magic or a miracle, but I can work the trick that it takes to make you immortal."

There were several minutes of silence. Julian waited anxiously, not knowing what to expect. He watched her face, searching for some reaction.

"Oh, Julian," she whispered. "Really? You are? This is wonderful." She turned, kneeling on the couch next to Julian. "Oh, but you're just teasing me. Prove it. Bite me." She turned her head, exposing her neck to him. "Show me your fangs."

"Alia, I'm telling you the truth. Here..." Julian pulled back his upper lip. As he extended his fangs, he watched Alia's eyes widen. She reached a finger toward his mouth. He let her get within in a hair's breadth of touching him; he snapped down, missing her finger, making her jump.

"Oh! You're mean!" She laughed at him. "Seriously though, would you do this for me? Can we do that now?"

"There's a lot we need to talk about before I make any decision about this." Julian looked at Alia, the hopeful look on her face fading. He leaned over and kissed her. "We should at least sleep on this. It's a big decision for both of us."

They went to bed, each wrapped in their own thoughts. Julian was in a deep sleep when he felt Alia touch him under the sheet. She occasionally woke him up this way, if she couldn't sleep; she said found him a much more pleasant way to find sleep than taking a sleeping pill.

He felt his cock growing hard as she stroked him slowly. He pretended to stay asleep, wondering how far she'd go. She began kissing his ear, working her way down his neck, pulling back the sheet and licking his nipples. Staying still was becoming hard; he was starting to squirm under her touch, his cock twitching in her touch.

Alia pulled the sheet down further, watching his cock grow larger as she worked it with her hand. Beads of pre-cum had started to form on the tip. He finally opened his eyes as she straddled his hips, rubbing his cock against her pussy with her hand. He could feel she was already wet; she must have been awake for quite some time.

"Sleepyhead. About time you woke up." She gently slipped him inside her, rocking her hips back and forth. Julian gently held her hips, letting her control the pace, letting her use him for the moment. She held her breasts as she rode his cock, rubbing the nipples with her palms, eyes closed.

Alia leaned forward, putting her hands on either side of Julian. She started pumping up and down faster on his cock. Julian grabbed one breast, reaching up to suck on the nipple. He found Alia's breasts intoxicating; frequently, she'd let him suck as long as he needed while she worked him with her hand, until he came, his face buried in her breasts.

As he sucked, he felt the urge to bite. Talking earlier about biting and showing his fangs had excited him, excited his desire to bite. His fangs brushed against the soft flesh of her breast; Alia felt the sharp sensation and looked down at him.

"Do it, Julian. Bite me." Her voice was deep and husky. "Do it now. Take me over to your side."

Julian was powerless to resist her and he let go of all his reserve; he sat up, turning them over on the bed, his cock still buried in Alia, rising above her. She looked up at him, her eyes glittering in the light from the window. He started thrusting into her, violently, his sexual desire and his desire to bite coming together in one firestorm of physical sensations. He pulled his lips back as his fangs extended. He could sense Alia's blood as it raced through her body. The only conscious thought he had was her heart was beating very fast, he would need to make sure she didn't lose blood too quickly. And then he stopped thinking and only felt.

Alia was watching him, wide-eyed, barely

moving beneath him. He felt infused with incredible power and strength. Wrapping his arms around her, he pulled her up, sitting back, holding her to his chest.

He rose up on his knees, thrusting up into Alia as she wrapped her arms around his neck, her legs around his hips. He grabbed her hips, ramming her down on his rigid cock as he continued thrusting up, harder and harder. He felt the power of his thrusts throughout her body; briefly, he wondered if he was hurting her. She was grunting with each thrust, the breath almost knocked out of her.

Julian ran his fangs along the tender skin of her neck, just below her ear, moving down to where her veins were closest to the skin, still thrusting rapidly into her. He savored the feel of her, the scent of her blood. For a vampire to bite during sex, to bite with abandon, was something indescribable. No mortal would ever understand the sensations combining the two acts created. It encompassed every nerve in his body, made every cell come alive with pure ecstasy.

Julian sunk his fangs into Alia's neck, felt the first spurt of blood on his tongue as his cock pounded into her body. The heat was building in his balls, shooting up the shaft of his cock as Alia's blood spurted into his mouth. He sucked on her neck as he had sucked on her breast, his cock exploding into her, shooting his hot load in her pussy.

He threw his head back, screaming, as his cock pumped into her, thrusting sharply, lifting her up by her hips and ramming her back down on his cock. Her blood ran down from his lips, coated his fangs. He was completely consumed by his physical sensations; had a bomb gone off in the next room he would not have noticed. He bent his head back to her neck, sucking deeply, drinking her blood as his cock pumped the last of his cum into her pussy.

Julian became aware of Alia trembling against him as her own feeble orgasm broke, dwarfed by the sensations of being bitten. He stopped sucking, panicked at the moment that he'd drained her. She was pale, but her heart was still beating strong.

Easing her back onto the bed, he looked at the wound. She's stopped bleeding, but she was unconscious. He shook her, no response. He slapped her lightly. Alia's eyelids fluttered. She took a sharp breath.

"Did you do it? Am I a vampire?" Her voice was weak, but excited. He smiled at her.

"No, there's one more thing. You need to drink my blood." Julian opened a vein on his wrist. He held her head gently, his wrist at her mouth. She sucked willingly, taking his blood into her mouth. Her eyes grew big as she sucked, swallowing greedily.

"Enough, Alia. You need to stop for now." He took his arm away. "You need to sleep now. You'll be very tired for some time. Rest. I'll be here when you wake up. If you get hungry, wake me. I'll feed you. It will take some time for you to learn what to do. This is why I wanted to wait. But it's too late. You're like me now." He kissed her forehead; her eyes were already starting to close. He pulled the covers over them, nestling her in his arms. He kissed her again. She was asleep.

Something was terribly wrong. Julian woke to thrashing on the bed, hands pulling at him, sharp nails in his throat. He struck out before even opening his eyes, hitting soft flesh. Sitting up, he saw Alia crouched naked at the foot of the bed, lips pulled back in an animal snarl, her eyes that deadly flat black he had seen only one time before. Francesca's face, distorted by the same snarl, flashed in his mind. She was bleeding from a cut on her cheek, presumably from him striking her.

Julian sat up. "Francesca..." Alia snarled, a cold vicious sound. Were it possible, Julian's blood would have run cold. He struggled free of the bed linens, trying to decide what to do, how to control her. Before he could make any move though, she jumped off the bed and with remarkable speed, ran out of the bedroom. Julian scrambled across the bed, reaching the bedroom door just as he heard the outer apartment door slam against the wall.

Naked, he ran down the hall to the outer door, flying naked into the hall. He caught just a glimpse of Alia at the end of the corridor, turning the corner. There was a growl, sounds of a struggle and a woman's scream, which ended in horrible gurgling sounds. Julian heard other building tenants shouting; he backed into the apartment, closing the door.

Julian dressed quickly and left the apartment. The scene around the corner of the corridor was gruesome; an elderly lady was on the floor, surrounded by tenants in their pyjamas. Blood pooled beneath her; her throat had been torn out. People were shouting, someone was trying to stop the massive bleeding, holding a towel to the woman's neck. But Julian, practiced in the art recognizing the dead, looked at the woman's eyes; there was no life there to save.

Sirens outside signaled the arrival of the emergency crew. Julian back away from the scene, heading down the emergency stairs rather than be seen by anyone. He knew it was Alia who had done this. He also knew he had created another terrible rogue vampire; once he was again responsible for destroying.

It took him almost a week to find Alia. He scanned the papers and the internet, trying to find a pattern in the murders he read about. Being unfamiliar with the city, he was at a loss in tracking her. He was frustrated and exhausted from the endless searching.

One night, as he drifted through the streets trying to catch her scent, he found he was on the block where her gallery was located. He'd been watching her apartment; she had never returned. The gallery had a closed sign in the window; it looked neglected, dark, and disordered.

Julian sent his mind into the gallery, sensing a terrible presence and the smell of death. He materialized inside, wary, on edge.

"Alia," he called her name. In response, he heard a low growl. She was crouched in the corner by the back door. She stood, wearing mismatched clothing, some torn, all of them dirty and covered with blood. Her hair was matted, caked with dirt and more blood. Her fingernails, those perfectly manicured nails he remembered her tracing patterns on his chest, were broken and bleeding. She looked like a demon from hell.

She launched herself at him. Julian anticipated her attack; he swiftly moved out of her way, spinning behind her, grabbing her around the neck, throwing her to the floor. He hoped she was not as strong as he was; again, as with Francesca, he knew he would be faster.

They fought for control, Alia spitting and growling, clawing at Julian's throat. He finally restrained her hands, sitting on her chest while she kicked her legs, pounded him on the back with her knees, trying to knock him loose. He wanted more than anything not to kill her. He tried to send his mind to hers but was hit with a wall of chaos, dark images soaked in blood. He kept trying, thinking this was why he'd failed with Francesca; he'd never had time to try to help her.

"Alia, it's Julian. It's me. Can you understand me?" She looked at him, her eyes that black he'd grown to hate. His mind was straining against hers when he felt a tiny flicker, a scream of pain from her mind. Alia's voice was calling to him, begging him for help.

"Try to come back, Alia, fight this! I know you can. You're strong! Fight your way back." He focused his mind on hers. As he watched her face, her eyes suddenly lost their black color; they became the glowing red he knew his became, when he fed. A tiny flame of hope lit in his chest.

"Julian... help me." Alia's voice was nothing more than a croak. "Please, kill me. I cannot stand this.

"Fight it, Alia. I'll help you." Julian searched her eyes, begging her, willing her to fight.

"I can't. This is... you need to end this. I can't stand the pain; the constant need to kill. It's terrible, it hurts so badly. I need to kill more; I need to kill now! Please end this... I can't... please, Julian, if you love me..." Julian watched as Alia's eyes began to shift, the glowing red fading, being replaced by solid black. "Please, Julian. I love you. But kill me... now!"

Alia began fighting against him again. He knew there was nothing else he could do. The Alia he'd known, and loved, was gone.

With one quick move, he tore across her throat with his nails, severing her jugular vein. Her blood ran crimson over the floor of the gallery, soaking into the wooden floor. Julian held her down as she struggled against him, watching her face.

For one brief instant, her eyes returned to their own startling clear blue. She looked up at him, unable to speak, but with a look of gratitude on her face. She smiled briefly and then closed her eyes. Her body relaxed and he knew she was gone.

Julian took the next flight back to New York. He left the airport and went directly to his Uncle at the Melosy Clan home. There was no one else he wanted to see, and he knew now he needed to tell Samuel what had happened, what he had done. And he needed to find an explanation.

Julian went directly from the airport to the Melosy Clan apartments at Dakota. Julian hadn't been to Dakota since before his search for Francesca, earlier that month. Where he had been hesitant before to talk to Samuel about Francesca, to admit he'd made some kind of horrible mistake, he now felt an overwhelming desire for Samuel's advice and counsel.

Julian had been closer to Samuel for most of his life. Samuel was very old; powerful and strong, hundreds of years of knowledge and experience guiding him as he ruled over the clan. He had tried to teach Julian, but being young and cocky, Julian was not always inclined to listen to Samuel. However, now, with two dead women—two dead rogue vampires he'd created—he knew Samuel was the only one he could turn to.

Samuel greeted Julian warmly, engulfing him in a hug. "It's good to see you Julian. You have been missed here, not only by me, but by the rest of the clan. Even your father expressed some interest in your absence." Julian's father, Eric, had shown less and less interest in Julian over the decades. But this was not the time for Julian to explore family differences and long-buried resentments.

"Samuel, I need your help. Something terrible has happened." Samuel looked at Julian's grief stricken face. He put his arm around Julian's shoulder and led him to the apartment's sitting area. It was furnished in Samuel's favorite style; Julian jokingly referred to it as "New Orleans Bordello," something of a cliché, a stereotypical vampire's decorating style. The walls were painted deep crimson red, the draperies were thick tapestries, and every piece of over-stuffed furniture was covered in velvet.

But for Julian, it was comforting to be among such familiar surroundings. He settled into a big wing chair facing the fireplace.

"Would you like something to drink? I have fresh stock, very nice. Would you like a glass?" Samuel offered Julian a glass of deep red blood, not synthetic. Samuel had connections that provided a regular supply of fresh, whole blood. The synthetic blood that had been developed to keep them from having to constantly feed on mortals was a poor substitute for the real thing. Samuel kept a supply of real blood at the Dakota; he said he was too old, and too smart, to have to rely on hunting to feed.

Julian took the glass, swirling the deep crimson liquid around in the cut crystal goblet. He took a sip; it was absolutely the freshest blood he'd had, outside of a living mortal. Samuel watched him closely as Julian took another drink.

"Very good. You need your strength; you're looking pale. Now, what do you need to talk about?" Samuel settled into the chair across from Julian.

Julian took a deep breath. He decided to start at the beginning, or the beginning in this whole tragedy Samuel was aware of, at least.

"Do you remember when I was looking for a girl, about a month or so ago? I'd asked if anyone had seen her."

Samuel nodded. "Yes. I thought you'd fallen in love. And then, nothing... you never asked again nor said you found her." Samuel looked thoughtful for a moment, gazing into the fire. He looked up at Julian with a serious expression.

"This was about the same time of those gruesome murders. Is there a connection between them?"

This was the reason, Julian decided, that Samuel was the leader of the clan. He was astute and perceptive and without needing to read minds could understand the bigger picture.

"Yes. She was the one who killed those people. And it was because of me that she killed... of what I made her." Julian looked at the floor.

"Did you turn her?" Samuel leaned forward in his chair. "Julian, did you make her into a vampire?"

Julian nodded, too ashamed to even say the words. "Oh, Julian. What a terrible thing to have happen." Samuel's voice was full of concern. "You do know though, why this happened?"

Julian looked up, shaking his head. "No. I assumed I did something wrong, that I forgot something, didn't give them enough of my blood... some misstep along the way."

"Them"? There is more than one vampire like this that you've created?" Samuel looked closely at Julian. "Just how many times have you done this, Julian?"

"Twice. There are—were—only two women." Julian looked at Samuel, seeing concern and worry in the other man's face. "The other was in Sweden. She is dead now, as well as Francesca."

"This is why I've told you to come to me before you do certain things. There is a great deal you do not understand about us—about the Melosy—even though we are your clan," Samuel sighed, suddenly looking old and tired.

"Julian, let me tell you why this has happened. You know we are different, that the Melosy possess certain abilities that give us—advantages—over other vampires. But those differences also make certain things more difficult for us. One of those is creating a vampire from a female mortal, especially once we're physically attracted to or in the midst of, shall we say, a close encounter. I assume with both women you were either very sexually attracted and in love with them, or were having sex with them?"

"Yes." Julian hesitated. He was both ashamed and embarrassed to admit the circumstances. "I was. Francesca... I wanted to spend eternity with her. I loved her. She was the perfect woman. Alia wanted to me to bite her, wanted to become a vampire. I bit her while we were having sex. I did love her as well, but not as deeply as Francesca."

Samuel sighed. "We have an additional burden as Melosy. We need to exert even more control than most vampires. Biting another vampire during sex is one thing; biting a mortal during sex is another. Feeding on a mortal is one thing; turning them into a vampire is another. The differences in us that make the Melosy able to withstand sunlight are not accepted by all mortal bodies, especially if we are in love with them and are in a highly aroused state when we bite them. Apparently, our body chemistry changes even more when we're in love, something that other vampires don't experience; apparently, not all vampires experience love. Unfortunate creatures. It's not completely understood, just as it's not completely understood why we can withstand some amount of sunlight." Samuel took a drink of his blood before continuing.

"At any rate, as you've seen, biting a mortal in that state sends them into what we've termed cumlandra, a dark desperate state for mortals, something they are unable to tolerate or control. There have been instances of mortals throughout history—who mortals call psychopaths or serial killers—who have been in cumlandra. They are driven to kill, not only to feed, but by the simple desire to destroy life. They are tormented creatures." Samuel waved his hand. "But you, my dear Julian, have seen that all too closely."

Julian struggled to understand what he'd heard. There were so many questions, but he was unsure where to start.

"But I've had sex with women, women I've bitten, and they didn't go into this state...this cumlandra. Why?"

"Think about the last woman you had sex with that you bit that didn't suffer this fate. What was different about that encounter?"

Samuel tilted his head, waiting for an answer.

"There was a girl in Paris, on my layover to Sweden. There were other girls in Sweden, other than Alia," Julian frowned. "I never knew their names. I met them, had sex and bit them...and fed. But that was all...that's as far as it went."

"You formed no attachment to them, had no feelings for them other than the purely physical desires of sex and feeding. You never even asked their names; you viewed them solely as objects... very pleasurable objects, but objects nonetheless. When you view a mortal woman as more than an object, as a love interest, then you've crossed a line and apparently started a chemical process that, if they're bitten, leads to cumlandra. You don't even need to continue the process of turning them, of feeding them your blood to produce this state; they would have become dangerous without that step. However, if you had taken too much blood, obviously they would have died and feeding them saves them. They were damned the minute you pierced their flesh, Julian. Damned by your feelings for them."

Julian's head ached. This was all too much to try to understand. "So I'm never going to have someone to spend eternity with? I'm going to be alone forever?"

"There are ways around this. If you find a mortal with whom you wish to spend eternity, who wishes to become one of us, simply have another clan member turn her. She will become like us, without going into cumlandra."

"You can also learn to dream walk, to enjoy

the pleasures a mortal woman who you care about has to offer—to love her if you will—without turning her or sending her into cumlandra, but still enjoy the exquisite pleasures of biting her during sex. Not all mortal women wish to become vampires and we can't turn every woman we love." Samuel laughed. "If we did, we'd end up with a harem over the centuries."

Julian rubbed his forehead. "So you're saying I can enter women's dreams and interact with them there? Women that I care about?"

"Well, you're able to read thoughts, yes? Enter their minds, plant suggestions?" Samuel's eyes grew bright as he talked. "It's similar, only a little more involved. To enter their subconscious while they're dreaming takes a little more finesse to keep from waking them. You need to be very careful that they do not wake up if you are having sex and begin to bite them. They will go into cumlandra, if they wake up. You can have all the sex you want with them in their dreams and if they wake up, you just keep having sex. But once you start to bite them, you must make sure they remain asleep." Samuel's voice was grave. "If they awake while you are biting them, they will most likely go into cumlandra. You need to maintain control."

Julian was overwhelmed. "I think I'll just give up women, or finding someone... or maybe sex altogether."

Samuel laughed. "No, Julian, you will not. It's nearly impossible for us to give up the pleasures of sex, either with our own kind or with the delicate flowers of the mortal race. We just need to exert extra care and caution. And you need to learn not to give your heart to every woman you desire or sleep with." Samuel sighed, his look distant. "I sometimes envy vampires from other clans; they don't carry this heavy burden. It's taken its toll on many of us over the centuries, those who do not pay attention to the advice given them." They were quiet for a moment, both gazing into the flickering fire.

"But don't be too sad. You're young; you will learn. There are thousands of women ahead of you in your life that you will enjoy. Just remember: you need to listen to your elders, to stop being such a cocky young bastard and realize we're here to help you."

Julian looked at Samuel, startled by his words. He saw Samuel smiling at him. Julian smiled, for the first time since he'd arrived. "Yes, Uncle. I promise to listen from now on."

"Good. Now, let me get you another drink. And we can talk about more pleasant things."

Julian left the Melosy Clan apartment several hours later, walking home in the twilight, calmer than he had been in weeks. He had a better understanding of what had happened, or at least he thought he did. It still made his head spin to think about what Samuel had explained. But he was excited by the idea of dream walking.

On the way to his apartment, he did find a pretty young thing, waiting on the curb for her boyfriend. She'd asked him if he had the time; he said he did. Julian made a point of not asking her name as he bent to bite her neck, taking her, standing up, in a doorway down an alley. She was sweet and pliant, hardly more than a mouthful.

His cock became instantly hard and huge as he bit and without hesitation he pulled up her skirt, tearing her panties way, pushing her against the door, thrusting up into her rapidly, one hand on her ass as she raised her leg, his fingers in the cleft between her cheeks. He pumped hard and fast, the sweet taste of her blood feeding his desire as it fed his body.

As he came, as his cock pumped his hot load into her waiting pussy, he threw back his head, crying out with each sharp thrust, an animal sound of pure pleasure from deep in his chest, the sound echoing down the alley. Every cell in his body seemed to be coming at once; even though the whole encounter took only minutes, his whole body felt ecstatic.

He left her, dazed but smiling, trying to straighten her clothes. He washed her mind clean of the encounter and briefly hoped her boyfriend wouldn't be too upset at finding her, fully satisfied, when he finally arrived.

Julian's apartment was as he had left it weeks before. He stopped only briefly, collecting his luggage from the foyer where it has been delivered and changing clothes. He couldn't face a night alone here yet. He left, wandering aimlessly about the city.

He eventually found himself at Donnie's, a local bar he liked. He walked in, the place fairly quiet. Julian sat in a corner booth, asking the waitress for a glass of scotch. He sometimes drank alcohol, mostly to be sociable with mortals, occasionally for the slight buzz it gave him, and he had acquired over the decades a taste for better quality single-malt scotch. He did understand for mortals the experience of drinking alcohol was quite different. He'd fed on drunken mortals, tasting whatever was in their system, either drugs or alcohol. There was never a lasting effect, just a hint of what they might be feeling.

Melissa was working behind the bar. She smiled as she brought Julian his drink. "Hey, stranger. I haven't seen you in ages. Where've you been?" She sat down across from him. Melissa was a stunning redhead, tall with a gorgeous figure. Julian had had a crush on her for a long time; she had a long-term boyfriend though. Melissa was one of the few women Julian respected enough not to interfere with her relationship by having sex with her, even though he desperately wanted to, and then washing her mind clean. He genuinely wanted her to be happy.

"I've been traveling. I just got back today. What have you been up to?" Julian really didn't want to get into detail and hoped Melissa wouldn't ask too many questions.

"Well, it's been hectic here, over the holidays. We're in that January lull now; everyone's partied hard during December and now made their New Year's resolutions to behave and cut back on the drinking. It lasts about two weeks and then they all come back. But we're enjoying the bit of quiet for the moment." Julian listened to her words but really wanted to read her mind. She was hiding something and he wanted to know what it was; he suspected it was about her boyfriend.

"And Joe, how's he?" Julian took a drink of scotch. Melissa dropped her eyes to the table.

"He's gone. We broke up, right before Christmas. Rotten timing; I'd gotten him a really nice gift, and now I'm left with a men's watch with his initials. Your name starts with J; you want a nice watch?" She smiled sadly. "Not sure what his reasons were, he gave the 'I need space' routine. I think that's bullshit. I think he found someone else."

Julian tried to keep a concerned look on his face, but he was secretly pleased. He wanted to sleep with Melissa very badly; his cock had decided now was a good time and was growing hard as they spoke. He wanted to manipulate her mind, wanted to put his own needs and desires, and his cock, into her, but he hesitated. Julian wanted only to sleep with Melissa; he didn't want to bite her, or he didn't want to bite her now. Samuel's words were playing in his head. He believed he understood what he could and could not do.

Against a tiny voice that said this wasn't a good idea, Julian sent the suggestion that Melissa should sleep with him. As he sent her this thought, she looked up, a playful glint replacing the sad look in her eye.

"Hey, I'm done here in a little while. Do you want to come back to my place? You can tell me about your trip, I can show you the engraved watch; we can see where things go." Melissa looked momentarily confused at hearing the words she was speaking. Julian had seen this before; if he didn't place the thought deep enough, some mortals could actually sense they were acting out of character. He pushed the thought a little harder. She instantly brightened and the confused frown left her face.

"I think that's a great idea, Melissa. Come get me when you're ready to leave." He watched her walk back behind the bar, her round ass in her tight jeans exciting him immensely. His cock was starting to make a bulge in his pants; he resisted the urge to reach down and rub himself. That wasn't proper behavior, even for a horny vampire.

Melissa's apartment was around the corner from the bar. They'd barely made it inside the door when they began simultaneously kissing and trying to tear off each other's clothes. He wondered if sub-consciously she had wanted this all along. His suggestion had been more or less inviting him back with the hint of sex; this woman obviously wanted him, and quickly. Julian gave up trying to understand.

Julian pulled Melissa's shirt over her head, revealing her full breasts in a lacy white bra. He cupped them, squeezing them hard in his hands, ramming his tongue into her mouth as she sucked on it. She was working her jeans down over her full hips, wiggling against Julian, rubbing against his cock with her body. She finally got them off her hips, breaking contact with his mouth as she kicked them off her legs. He caught a glimpse of a white thong, which he assumed would leave her perfect ass fully exposed. She returned to his mouth, biting his lips, sucking his lower lip with hers.

The bulge in his pants was huge, his erection very large, aching to be released. Melissa yanked the zipper down, stripping his pants to his ankles in one motion. She slid her body against his as she slowly stood, pushing her breasts against his cock, momentarily catching him between her full tits. Julian moaned at the contact, thrusting forward involuntarily at the contact.

"Would you like to fuck my tits, Julian? Do you want to rub your cock between them, feel how soft they are?" Melissa was half kneeling, half bending before him, the head of his cock between her breasts.

"Oh, God, yes." He could barely get the words out. The thought of rubbing his hard shaft between her breasts was almost too much. Melissa stood, taking him by the hand. She sat on the edge of the couch, Julian standing in front of her. She reached down and undid the hook at the front of her bra. To Julian, her breasts were perfect; round and firm, hard rose-colored nipples just out of his reach. But best of all, his cock was now between those breasts.

Melissa pressed her breasts together as Julian slid his cock between them, feeling the warmth of her velvety soft skin around his shaft. He pumped slowly up and down for a moment, watching his cock fucking her breasts, Melissa watching his cock slide up and down.

As he thrust up, Melissa bent her head, licking the tip of his cock, running her tongue under the sensitive underside of his cock. He held himself there, letting her take the crown of his dick into her mouth for a moment, sucking on just the head, and then pulling back from her. He thrust up again, Melissa taking more of his cock into her mouth this time, sucking briefly before he pulled back.

Julian watched her take his cock into her mouth on each upstroke as he continued to fuck her breasts. He started thrusting faster, wanting more of his cock in her mouth. She sensed what he wanted and let go of her breasts with her hands, freeing him from their soft confines.

Melissa took him fully in her mouth then, as he thrust the length of his shaft into her warm mouth. She swirled her tongue around his cock, sucking hard on his dick, taking his long shaft almost all the way into her mouth. He could feel the tip of his cock hitting the back of her throat.

Melissa apparently had some experience giving blow jobs; she was totally in control as she thrust him in and out of her mouth. She looked up at him with her large green eyes as he took her head in his hands. She'd started running the fingers of one hand over his balls, rubbing them, making him moan with pleasure. He wanted to fuck her; he really wanted to thrust himself unrelentingly into that mouth, watch her take his whole cock and pump his load into her, to watch her lick his cock with his come on her tongue, and then watch her swallow his load. But he didn't want to use Melissa; he wanted her to be satisfied as well.

Julian pulled out of her mouth, grabbing her shoulders and pulling her off the couch.

He reached down and pulled her thong away from her pussy, sticking his hand between her legs. She was practically dripping as he thrust his fingers into her. She cried out, rubbing against him.

"Fuck me, Julian. Right here, right now." She turned around, kneeling on the couch, her hands on the back, showing him that luscious ass, those perfect round cheeks, her swollen slit visible between her spread legs. She looked at him over her shoulder, smiling.

Julian pulled her thong away from her ass and out of her slit, the material soaked. He ran his hand over her pussy, her juices covering his fingers. He tickled her clit, making her squirm.

"Now, Julian! Now... I can't wait." Melissa wiggled her ass provocatively at Julian. "Stick it to me, Julian. Give me all you got, big boy!"

Julian grabbed her hips, thrusting into Melissa, ramming himself completely into her pussy, his balls against her ass. He held himself against her, twisting his hips back and forth, his cock filling Melissa completely. She pushed back against him, rubbing her hips up and down. The uncoordinated combination of their movements first made them giggle, but they quickly developed a rhythm, grinding against each other, enjoying the unusual but arousing sensations.

Julian reached around between Melissa's legs, finding her clit, rubbing and pinching the little button of flesh, feeling her buck against him. He rubbed harder, making her cry out. "Too hard?"

"No, do that again...do that harder." Julian

did as he was told; he pulled her clit, massaging it harder, roughly tugging it. Melissa cried out with each tug and pull, arching her back, pumping her hips sharply up and down against Julian's thighs. Julian could feel her pussy dripping on his hand.

Suddenly she screamed, rounding her back, her orgasm ripping through her. Julian felt her pussy contract around his cock, felt her squirting on his hand, hearing it hit the leather couch. She shuddered briefly beneath him. He was too taken by surprise to react. He kept rubbing her clit until she gently pushed his hand away.

"That was unexpected." Melissa was panting as she spoke. "Sorry. Sometimes that happens. Thanks. We're done now. Good night." Melissa looked at him over her shoulder. She laughed out loud.

"Sorry, just kidding. You should see the look on your face." Julian had never come across anyone like Melissa. He laughed at her cheeky sense of humor.

"You're in for it now, Melissa." He pulled her off the couch, turning her around to face him. He kissed her, grabbing her ass with his hands, pulling her against his aching cock, seeking to thrust it into her while standing, frustrated that he couldn't get the right angle.

"Where's the bedroom?" He growled against her. She motioned down the hall. With one motion, he picked her up, tossing her over his shoulder as he strode down the hall and found a bedroom, his hard cock sticking straight out in front of him, pointing the way. "This is the guest room," she panted against his back.

"I don't give a fuck. It's got a bed." He tossed her down on her back, spreading her legs and kneeling between them, his cock sticking out, harder than he could ever remember it being. He grabbed her hips, pulling her roughly up his hard thighs toward his cock, her pussy spread before him. Melissa's lips were parted, her breath coming in short gasps, watching Julian's huge cock poised to thrust into her.

With a sharp cry and one huge push, Julian thrust himself into Melissa's waiting pussy. He pulled back, and then began thrusting into her again and again, head back, mouth open, finally able to work his cock into her, to bury his dick in that wet hole.

He looked down at Melissa; she was holding her breasts in both hands. She'd licked her fingers and was rubbing her nipples, pulling and pinching the way Julian had worked her clit earlier. He had no intention of holding back now; he was slightly frustrated and although that usually irritated as well, he found he was enjoying this well-earned earned fuck.

Julian felt his balls filling with heat, his orgasm building, and nothing was going to stop him from pumping his load into her. He was grunting with each thrust, pounding her pussy. The heat of his orgasm was flooding up his shaft, bringing him to the edge of coming.

"Julian..." Melissa began. Julian scowled down at her.

"Not a word," he grunted. "Not one fucking word." He smiled, more of a grimace, but still a smile.

Melissa laughed as Julian panted in exertion. She reached down between his legs and grabbed his balls, stroking them rather aggressively. That was enough to send him over the edge.

With a final shout, his orgasm burst from his cock. Julian arched his back, straining to push his cock even further into Melissa, holding her to him by her hips, his body shaking with the effort. He thrust into her several times quickly, each time spurting more of his load into Melissa, filling her with his hot cum.

Julian's orgasm finally faded. He eased Melissa down off his cock, lying beside her on the bed. He gently stroked her hair as she ran her fingers down his chest, eventually both of them falling asleep.

Julian woke sometime later in the dark apartment, not sure of his surroundings. He looked down at the sleeping Melissa and remembered where he was. He smiled to himself, pulling her against his chest. As he was drifting off again, Samuel's words came back to him. He was instantly wide awake, wondering how successful he would be at dream walking.

With infinite care, he extended his mind to hers. He entered what he thought was a dream; none of the images he saw made any sense. He watched for a moment, entering further into the dream. Melissa was there, apparently dreaming of being on the beach. They were walking along the water, the sun shining down. He concentrated harder and suddenly she was talking to him. She reached out and touched his face, pulling him toward her. "I feel bad. I made sex hard for you. I should make that up to you." Julian was shocked; apparently, she felt bad about their evening together.

"It's okay..." he started to answer, but she pulled him toward her, kissing him hard. She grabbed his cock; he was already hard. She pulled him down on the sand of the beach; suddenly they were both naked. It appeared he couldn't control her dream but could only interact with her as her dream progressed. It was disconcerting; he was suddenly fucking her hard, hearing her scream as he pounded into her. He felt himself coming, excited by her thrashing beneath him.

He felt his fangs extending, suddenly wanting to bite and unable to control himself, but since he was in her dream, he realized he didn't need to. As she continued to arch beneath him, he sank his fangs into her long neck. He tasted her hot blood, felt himself coming, screaming into her neck as she convulsed beneath him, lost in the throes of her own orgasm.

Julian woke with a start, Melissa sleeping beside him. He was rock hard, thrusting his hips against Melissa's ass, his cock rubbing against her, his face buried in her hair. He rolled onto his back as she continued sleeping. He was relieved she was still asleep; he was rather embarrassed by trying to hump her in her sleep. But his hard-on ached.

Julian got dressed and wrote a quick note for Melissa, explaining he had an early morning appointment and that he'd call her later, after finding her cell phone and memorizing the number. He left his number as well and walked out into the night. He quickly found a woman on the sidewalk, pulling her into an alley, pushing her against the wall, fucking her from behind as he groped her breasts. He came quickly, releasing his pent up frustration. He washed her mind and sent her on her way, walking quickly to his own apartment, letting himself in and collapsing into his own bed.

Julian slept heavily through the following day. He awoke disoriented, finally recognizing it was the following night after he'd been with Melissa. The flight from Sweden, meeting with Samuel... then spending time with Melissa: his day had been exhausting. He showered, dressed and tried calling Melissa; the call when to voicemail. He tried calling Donnie's but no one had seen her; she'd missed her shift.

Worried, Julian walked to her apartment. He knocked; there was no answer. He sent his mind into the apartment, finding Melissa inside. He materialized through the door and found her still sleeping. He tried to wake her; she was groggy but coherent. He got her up, gave her some juice he found in the refrigerator and she started acting normally. They talked for a while; she said she thought she was getting the flu, tried calling in to work but had fallen back asleep. She said she felt tired again. Would he come lay down with her until she fell asleep?

Julian took her to her own bed, curling up beside her as she nestled in the covers. She fell asleep with her head on his chest. He waited until he thought she would be sound asleep and then sent his mind into hers. He entered a dream, this one very different from her early sunny dream of the beach. This world was dark and chaotic, the ground rocky and strewn with garbage. He saw someone far ahead of him, someone he didn't recognize. Then she turned. It was Melissa.

Her lips were pulled back in an ugly snarl. Julian recoiled from her, horrified by what he saw; he barely recognized her. He started to run, but time seemed to fold over on itself; in an instant Melissa was on him. They fell to the rocky ground; Julian felt rocks cutting his skin, but Melissa seemed impervious to the sharp stones. She was trying to tear at his throat and for a moment, memories of Francesca and Alia washed over him. But this was only Melissa's dream. He fought her off, rolling on top of her, grabbing her shoulders. There was another glitch in the dream. He looked down and Melissa was dead; he'd broken her neck.

Julian pulled back from her dream, disengaging his mind. He sat up in her bed, Melissa rolling away from him, her head lolling at an unnatural angle on her shoulders. Julian looked down in horror; Melissa was dead, her neck broken.

Julian covered the distance between her apartment and the Dakota in minutes, using every power at his command to find Uncle Samuel. A clan member answered the door; Julian pushing past him to his Uncle's room. Samuel rose as Julian flung the door open.

“Julian! What is wrong? Are you all right?” Julian stumbled into the room, collapsing in the same chair he’d occupied the day before. Samuel sat down across from him. “What has happened?”

“I’ve killed a woman, an innocent woman this time. Not a rogue vampire. I don’t know what I did wrong.” Julian was close to tears.

“Start with the beginning. Tell me everything you did, starting from the moment you met her.” Samuel sat forward in his chair, a deeply worried look on his face.

Julian began at the beginning, from meeting Melissa at Donnie’s through finding her, apparently sick, at her apartment. Samuel listened quietly. When Julian was finished, Samuel sat back.

“Julian, when you were biting her, were you certain she was asleep?” Samuel’s eyes were serious, waiting for Julian’s answer.

“I believe so. How could she not be asleep if I was in her dream?” Julian was confused.

“Julian, this was your first attempt at dream walking. You chose a woman you knew, that you had feelings for, correct?” Julian nodded.

“I believe she was not dreaming, that she was awake when you bit her and again when you killed her. You were not in control. You said there were instances when the dream seemed to jump or skip. When you’re dream walking, even though we know that dreams sometimes make no sense, you should be able to control them, to keep the flow of the dream running smoothly. The jumps—the glitches, as you call them—are you losing control.”

Samuel arose, getting them each a glass of blood. Julian took the goblet, swirling the liquid but not drinking.

"You need to be in total control when you dream walk: total control at all times. It takes practice and it takes knowing when to back off, if necessary. You lost control and a girl is dead. This is regrettable."

Julian looked at Samuel. "What do I do now?"

"Well, you take some time to reflect on the past and learn from your mistakes. You practice on women you have no connection to, that you feel nothing for. Walk in their dreams, remain in total control, learn how and when to leave their dreams. It's not something you can do perfectly the first time. I thought you realized that. But in any event, don't attempt this with someone you care about. At least not until you are very good at it."

Julian left the Dakota, walking home. He had no intention of getting close enough to any woman to even consider walking in her dream. He was going to become cold and heartless, taking what he wanted, feeding and fucking with no thought of love or even caring about who he was with.

ABOUT THE AUTHOR

Readers: I want to expand a few of the stories to see where the characters can be explored further. If there are any of the stories that you would like to read more about again, I'd love to hear from you!

Visit my blog at www.shalabreece.com

Join my newsletter for free exclusive previews http://www.shalabreece.com/in

Follow me on Twitter at http://www.twitter.com/shalabreece

Like my page on Facebook at http://www.facebook.com/shalabreece

Discover my books at major ebook retailers everywhere.

www.ingramcontent.com/pod-product-compliance
Lightning Source LLC
LaVergne TN
LVHW091149080826
845145LV00008B/2312

* 9 7 8 1 6 2 3 2 7 5 7 7 8 *